Mary Wings began her writing career with *She Came Too Late*, winner of the *City Limits* Best Novel of the Year Award, and first published by The Women's Press in 1986. *She Came Too Late* launched the bestselling career of intrepid detective Emma Victor, and was followed by *She Came in a Flash* (The Women's Press, 1988) and *She Came by the Book* (The Women's Press, 1995).

Mary Wings has also written the bestselling gothic detective novel, *Divine Victim* (The Women's Press, 1992), which won the Lambda Literary Award in 1993. Her books have been translated into Dutch, German, Japanese and Spanish. Mary Wings has been nominated for the Raymond Chandler Fulbright in Mystery and Spy Fiction and lives in San Francisco, California with various cats.

D1180882

Also by Mary Wings from The Women's Press:

She Came Too Late (1986)
She Came in a Flash (1988)
Divine Victim (1992)

MARY WINGS
SHE CAME BY THE BOOK
THE THIRD EMMA VICTOR MYSTERY

First published by The Women's Press Ltd, 1995
A member of the Namara Group
34 Great Sutton Street, London EC1V 0DX

Copyright © Mary Wings 1995

British Library Cataloguing-in-Publication Data
A catalogue record for this book is available from the British Library

ISBN 0 7043 4432 7

Phototypeset in Times by Intype, London
Printed and bound in Great Britain by
BPC Paperbacks Ltd, Aylesbury, Bucks

Contents

Prologue 1

Chapter One: History 2

Chapter Two: Iambic Pentameter 13

Chapter Three: Genre 26

Chapter Four: Appetizers 36

Chapter Five: Speech 49

Chapter Six: Potatoes 58

Chapter Seven: Diet Fresca 68

Chapter Eight: Wrong Number 79

Chapter Nine: Red Dora's Bearded Lady Café 87

Chapter Ten: Dark Nativity 98

Chapter Eleven: Preservation 111

Chapter Twelve: Bad Housekeeping 124

Chapter Thirteen: Cleaning and Sleep 135

Chapter Fourteen: I Dream of Deborah 140

Chapter Fifteen: Tracy's Terrain 150

Chapter Sixteen: The Key to Renquist Falkenberg 158

Chapter Seventeen: Blind Date 168

Chapter Eighteen: Vaulting Fresca 179

Chapter Nineteen: Riot 186

Chapter Twenty: Twin Peaks 192

Chapter Twenty-One: What Eleanor Roosevelt Said 196

This book is for
Eric Garber
and
Laurie Liss.
Friends indeed.

Acknowledgements

Many thanks to my editor Kathy Gale, who, in pushing us both beyond our limits, had a marvelous effect on this story, and became a friend.

And to the women who sheltered me behind thick stone walls during the hottest European summer since 1863: Andrea Achtatz, Evelyne Bögli-Huber, Karin Van Elderen, Kade Hug, Conny Scherrer, Gabriella Stammbach and Elly de Waard.

To book antiquarian, Celia Sack, who knows what vellum feels like.

And finally to my three mentors on Bernal Hill: Joan Holden, Kris Kovick and Ruby Rich, who have given me sound ideas on how life and writing should be done.

History there = is no disaster because = Those who make history =
Cannot be overtaken = As they will make = History which they
do = because it is necessary = That every one will = Begin to
know that = They must know that = History is what it is =
Which it is as they do =

Gertrude Stein

Howard Blooming Lesbian and Gay Memorial Archive

Gala Dinner

TRACY PORT – Executive Director of the Archive
RENQUIST FALKENBERG – City Supervisor
DEBORAH DUNTON – President of the Board and couples counselor
ALLEN BOONE – Assistant Curator
HELEN THOMAS – Mystery author and keynote speaker
BERNIECE ABLE – Board Member and Pulitzer poet
CARLA RIBERA – Board Member and fashion photographer
LARRY BOZNIAN – painter of Archive mural
FRESCA ALCAZON – Gertrude Stein expert
ROSEANNA BAYNETTA – donor; security expert
LEE TURGO – donor; chiropractor
~~**FRANCES COHEN** – physician and researcher~~ *canceled*
EMMA VICTOR – donor

Prologue

As a lesbian I never thought that I would mind another woman wearing *the same* dress to a big event. But the woman was Tracy Port, and the dress looked so very good on her, even while she was being poisoned at my feet.

My eyes unwillingly watched Tracy's body convulse. I felt guilty. Not because I'd felt bad about Tracy Port wearing the same dress as me to the Howard Blooming Lesbian and Gay Memorial Archive Dinner. And not because, even when dying, I felt she looked better in it than I did. But because somehow I thought the disaster that had ruined the dinner, that had taken Tracy's life, was all my fault.

I tried not to focus on the death mask taking over Tracy's features. But we were all transfixed, staring at Tracy clutching her throat, the black sequins of our dress blinking like a few thousand blinded raccoons. On the marble floor, the hem of my dress was rising to reveal the muscularly developed legs of the Executive Director of the Lesbian and Gay Memorial Archive. Spectacular legs which had taken her over many a finish line. And on publicity jogs with politicians like the potential Senator, Renquist Falkenberg. But Tracy had been dancing with an invisible demon of death and now the dance was done. Tracy lay at my feet. Dead.

Get a grip, Emma Victor. Figure out just exactly what you're doing here. And why someone is tugging on a box at the end of your arm. A box you're supposed to be guarding with your life. It started with an errand. It has ended in death. Hold on tight.

Chapter One

History

The fog was spilling over the edge of the hills like a cloud from a bad Aladdin's lamp. It poured through the split in Twin Peaks and filled the Castro Valley, so thick it blanked out the 'C' and the 'A' on the sign of that landmark plaster movie palace, the Castro Theater. Only a bright pink 'STRO' shone through the mist, gilding with neon the happy queer people who roamed the streets buying chocolate chip cookies, renting videos and browsing in Cliff's Hardware Store. Couples clutched each other in the fog and laughed. San Francisco, where it never rains but the streets are always wet.

David Stimpson and Howard Blooming's house was an old Victorian homestead bought in the mid-seventies like so many other dwellings here. With a lot of disposable income on hand, white gay men had bought up the properties which surrounded the Castro Theater. Slowly they displaced the working-class Irish who were escaping queers and crime by moving to the suburbs. The new residents turned the formerly beige and white Victorian houses into multi-colored gay homesteads with perfectly pruned rosebushes and flower boxes up front. Not a dead leaf dangling. The property values shot up sky high. Gaylandia was a realtor's dream.

I banked the wheels against the curb of a steep hillside and struggled against gravity to open the car door. Stepping into that cool shroud of fog I shivered and pulled up the collar of my leather jacket. I looked up at the familiar house, its numerals shining in solid brass.

I wondered how long David would stay this time. Then I didn't wonder any more. A big 'FOR SALE' sign swung on a pointy-topped post in the middle of a recently tidied garden. David was selling the place. That was all right with me. History could move on, as far as I was concerned. Other people could live in the past, I thought. But that's only what I thought then. I had forgotten that we are sometimes a sum of things that have happened in the past. And that the past could dictate your future like it was written in stone.

Howard Blooming had lived in this house with his lover David Stimpson. Originally a mild mannered chemist, he'd had the honor of being our country's first elected gay official. And its first martyr.

A horseshoe arch led into a portico where a bas-relief had been lovingly revealed and restored. Howard Blooming had spent every week for a month with dental tools and hand-held acetylene torches removing the paint off the wooden carving. A moon, sun and star had been gilded on a background of blue, its original meaning lost with the many papers that had been destroyed when City Hall burned in the San Francisco earthquake of 1906. A lamp shed a sad refracted glow through beveled glass across the kind of porch where men and women would share a pristine kiss in times gone by. Or women and women.

Howard Blooming's kisses had never been pristine. As his press secretary I had run interference for the numerous affairs Howard had indulged in as a successful politician. It wasn't always easy keeping secrets from David, but it was absolutely necessary. He had always suspected an affair between Howard and his protégé, Renquist Falkenberg. David was a bit paranoid and we handled him with kid gloves.

Earlier that day I had called the number indicated on the digital display on my pager. I'd heard the voice I hadn't heard in years, a voice that made time stop in its tracks.

'Emma, it's David Stimpson. I just got in from Paris. I need some help. I called Willie and she said to call you.'

Willie was my employer, a lawyer who had handled some of Howard and David's affairs. 'So you want me to come over, David?' I asked reluctantly.

After Howard had been assassinated and a suitable period of mourning had passed, David Stimpson had made himself available for public appearances in Howard's name. He had slipped on the mantle of professional widow like a simple black sheath. The Widow of Howard Blooming was no mean position in Fairyland but it wasn't an act I admired. I knew that David had loved Howard though. Being a professional widow had been fulfilling but it hadn't made up for the loss. And when Renquist Falkenberg's light cast a big shadow over little David Stimpson, David had eventually moved away to Paris.

'Yes and come quickly, Emma,' his voice had caught in his throat. 'I think – I think someone has been following me –'

Now, standing at David's door I watched that familiar, thin shadow loping down a long hallway of time through the glass. The deadbolt slid open, the brass knob turned, the door revealed David Stimpson. He was a little older, a lot grayer and a wilted version of his old topiaried mustache curled over his lips.

'Emma!' The small eyes were wary and he hung back; we would not be engaging in the California hug routine. David and I had never engaged in niceties, not after Howard died.

'Thanks for coming, Emma.'

'That's okay, but I haven't got long.' I knew David could be long-winded and he looked upset. 'What can I do for you?'

'I hate it here, Emma.' Oh, God, it was the *white whine*. I got ready for the long exposition, all the details David would tell me about his life that I didn't want to hear before he got to the climax, the errand he wanted me to run for

4

him. I just wanted to get the errand done, preferably in time to get home, put on my tux and watch my girlfriend slink into the black sheath I was carrying in a Macy's box.

'I'm finally packing up, Emma,' he said. 'I thought I would be able to return after twenty years, but I still haven't got the heart for it.'

'David, can we cut to the chase here?' But David, ever the retail queen, was eyeing the box from Macy's. Inside was the black sequined dress for Frances, her first after-five acquisition in years. The low-cut back was going to frame the downy skinned flanges of Frances' shoulder-blades to perfection.

'You got a dress at *Macy's*?'

I nodded.

'I *never* shop at Macy's anymore.'

'I'm trampled, David.' But I was also curious. 'By the way, may I enquire as to how much you are asking for the house?'

'Two million.'

Two million.

'Two million? What is this, Pacific Heights?'

'It's the only extant example of Queen Anne architecture of the period, not to mention the – ' The little lips tightened defensively and he began over again. 'I've got a two million offer. Firm.'

'Two million. Mazeltov. Who's buying?'

'It was an anonymous offer. Willie's handling it.' He sighed dramatically. 'It will be good to get away. Away from all the memories – '

'Could we linger in the present for just a moment David? Or do you want to turn back the clock and camp out at the one second that changed history – '

'You robbed me of the only man I loved.'

Here we went again. It would always be the same for this man.

'David, take the nails out of your hands and climb down

off the cross. It wasn't *my* job to protect Howard, David. I was his *publicist*.'

'The death threats *had* been coming on a regular basis, Emma. Ever since Howard started his campaign for the rights of lesbian and gay schoolteachers. I still don't see why he had to be in the public eye so much of the time. And that nightmare baptism – '

'Oh, David – ' But there wasn't anything left to say. We all knew the facts of twenty years ago. They weren't going to change. The Universal Community Church baptism had been the incendiary event that had set off the right-wing fundamentalists. The Church had sponsored a multi-denominational baptism of infants from parents of all sexual persuasions. The truly rainbow event was joyous for the San Francisco community. It had been even better for the press.

The right-wing fundamentalists had gotten wind of the event and had staged a massive, vicious protest. One of their key organizers, Jeb Flynne, later killed the leading figurehead present at the baptism. Killed Howard Blooming. That's how it all worked in David Stimpson's mind. And it was still all my fault. My grievous fault.

'Emma, I begged you not to let Howard do that speech after the baptism. He would have listened to you but you said *nothing*. It was more than bad judgement. It was *negligence*.'

I couldn't summon up the energy for anger. David was still trying to pass on his guilt. He'd flounced off in a huff, when Howard had refused to be frightened off from delivering his speech and he'd stayed away for a month. Howard had been killed before they made up. I was the one who'd held Howard in my arms as he was dying, I was the one who'd heard his final words. It had made great press. David had missed the opportunity to become the Jackie Kennedy of queers.

'I just want rid of the journals – '

'Journals? What journals?'

'You can *have* them.'

6

'*What* journals?'

'You can *all* have them! You, Renquist, the fucking *community* – you took Howard – ' David's face was crumpling now, his skin wrinkling into self pity.

'We didn't take Howard. Howard gave himself.' But as I was pontificating, a rhythm started up in my head. The journals, the journals. Get him to tell you about the journals.

'I'm sorry, Emma. I just keep reliving it, over and over.' He smiled weakly. 'Guess I'm better off in Paris. C'mon.' He ushered me into their Victorian style parlor. In its former days it would have made Abigail Lincoln proud. But now, shorn of red brocade curtains, hand-knotted lace sheers and gilded mirrors, without its gold cupids poised on tiptoe, the room looked forlorn. An abandoned bordello.

The pano view, worth, it seemed, two million dollars, filled a bay window. The fog had wrapped around the Twin Peaks television tower like a big scarf. Lights glimmered over the gentle folds of hills. All kinds of friends and families would be coming home from work. Putting dinner in the microwave.

I looked around. This home had long gone. Rows of boxes were carefully labeled and organized.

'Emma, I want Howard's final journals housed at the Lesbian and Gay Archive.

'The *Howard Blooming* Lesbian and Gay *Memorial* Archive.' I said it gently.

'*What*?' David's body shuddered and a sad look crept over his face. 'I guess I *am* out of touch. In any event I want Howard's journals at the Archive. I mentioned it to Willie. She said you were going to the Gala dinner tonight.'

The journals. Howard Blooming's final diaries and David wanted to give them to the Archive. The diaries of Howard's last two years; the journals, which I knew he'd kept, but which David had insisted had disappeared.

I'd never trusted the story of their alleged disappearance. But I noticed David hadn't sold them to any journalists if he did have possession of them. Howard Blooming's jour-

7

nals. Who wouldn't want to hold them? Who wouldn't want to read them? Who hadn't been waiting for them for twenty years?

David left the room and returned with a faded, flowered hat box. From Macy's. Where David never shopped anymore. I looked at the box and wondered at the history it now held. Had it originally held a nubby wool sweater – didn't Howard prefer the Man of Aran look? A present, perhaps from David Stimpson to Howard Blooming, in some chilly season at the beginning of their relationship?

A twisted string handle was threaded through opposite sides of the box and rested on the lid. David looked at me a long time. Once I had the journals he would be rid of the final secrets of Howard Blooming, the secrets that might still haunt David Stimpson, the secrets he could probably sell to a publisher, naming his price in the booming lesbian and gay book market. Before he had a chance to wrestle with his conscience and lose I spoke up.

'It's the right thing to do,' I said.

'I made an appointment for you with Allen Boone, assistant Curator of the archive. He's delighted, of course.' David looked down at the box. 'The last diaries. And letters.' His voice was soft. 'And, uh, some personal clutter – memorabilia. It's all in there.'

My hands reached out and took hold of the package. It was evenly covered with a decade of dust. Something, like a marble, rolled across the floor of the box.

'There's something loose in there,' David grinned wanly. 'Howard tucked a few extra mementoes in, I guess. He was always so, so – disorganized.'

Howard's image as the faintly absentminded chemist had served him well. But he'd had a mind like a trap and he'd learned how to swing on the political ropes of San Francisco politics. I stared at the box in my hands. It was heavy. I tried not to smile.

'Oh, and there's one more thing, Emma. The most important thing. The journals may not be read until everyone who might have been mentioned in them has died. The box must be sealed, Emma. Sealed for sixty years. It was Howard's wish. I know I can trust you to see to it.'

I stepped out into the street with two boxes from Macy's. An old box with a faded pattern of twenty years ago, containing the final journals of Howard Blooming. The other, a more modern version, for the more modern type of lesbian that Frances was becoming. A lipstick lesbian. In a black sequined shift. The Howard Blooming box bumped on my hip. I shook it. Some kind of bead, or button was rolling around; a troubling, disturbing sound. Something loose inside a box that Howard wanted sealed for sixty years. My imagination ran wild with history and supposition. I stood for a moment, temptation and loyalty to Howard warring in my mind. I couldn't do it. I couldn't let Howard down now. I set off down the steep stairs, my mind drifting back to Howard Blooming's death.

Every politician fears assassination. Especially politicians like Howard, who were breaking such new ground. Howard had received death threats – phone calls and letters. We tried to keep the unsettling news from David. And more than a few of the facts.

The assassin, Jeb Flynne, had been a member of the Family Values Coalition. A group that believed that women were better left barefoot and pregnant, queers burned at the stake and white heterosexual males, that endangered group, should be armed to the teeth. Flynne had been arrested on the spot. He later committed suicide in jail. There were ridiculous rumors that Jeb Flynne was still alive, a demolition expert in Germany or peeling potatoes in Tangier perhaps, but there'd never been any evidence to substantiate the stories.

I stepped from under the canopy of the eucalyptus tree, glad to be out of the shadows. I gave a quick look around the street. Gentrified garages, Queen Anne's, stood majestically on the hillsides. I heard the historic cheers of Howard's people, our people, the whispered rumors about Jeb Flynne, as I held the box full of Howard's family skeletons. I looked up at the bay windows off the master bedroom. They'd been a hassle for the security guards. Howard had liked to take his coffee there in the morning in his Black Watch plaid flannel pajamas. I would brief him there. Ah, Howard.

Before he became political Howard used to spend all his time puttering around the house, in his workshop down in the basement with his Bunsen burners and test tubes. He had been a dedicated chemist but he gave it up for the chance to make history. Still, Howard was no saint. Howard had peddled pot in the sixties and maybe messed with LSD in the eighties.

And I knew, for example, that Laurie Leiss was Howard's cousin.

Those few people who had known it had forgotten. Conveniently or otherwise. Laurie Leiss, well known as a political cartoonist, had been a leading revolutionary in what some had thought was a revolution in 1972. At the height of the Vietnam War, any number of radicals had taken up the gun in the United States.

They'd built bombs. Robbed banks. And the violence in Laurie Leiss' cartoons had moved out of her strips and on to the streets.

Laurie Leiss was under investigation for a number of these acts. When a bomb tore up a brownstone in New York, her fingerprints had been found all over the apartment. Later *four counts* of murder were added after a botched bank robbery, which nevertheless netted five hundred thousand in cash.

But that was long, long before I started working for Howard. Long, long before Laurie Leiss had actually contacted Howard. Asking for money. That was something only Howard and I knew. And Laurie Leiss.

It was 1981 and Howard had been in office a year. A phone call came in on Howard's personal line. We never knew how she'd found the number. But I delivered the cash immediately. As Howard's Press Secretary I knew the value of getting Laurie Leiss out of his hair quickly and quietly. And without asking questions.

Howard had me deliver the twenty thousand dollars in cash in El Cerrito. Twenty-dollar bills banded together to fill a small suitcase. It was a hot day. And the person who was Laurie Leiss, or Laurie Leiss' agent approached me in the middle of a Supermart parking lot to pick it up. She wore a hat with a large brim and dark glasses. A shapeless nylon dress had billowed below her knees. She had walked quickly across the asphalt in flat shoes. A little woman with a big problem.

I looked up and down the street, feeling the presence of windows around me. Windows behind which people were making new secrets. Secrets to be kept for ever, secrets that would be destroyed. Bits of history, important to someone, doomed to disappear.

The mist was extending its clammy fingers, the stars failed against the fog and I realized I was leaving the Rainbow House for the last time. I was just arriving at the bottom of the stairs when a convertible, top down, tried to make it up the hill. The occupants were laughing, their faces a blur behind the windshield. The black man's arm was slung around what looked like a white drag queen, in a futile effort to keep him/her warm. I squinted.

Then their car had clutch trouble; I'd seen it often enough before on a hillside in San Francisco. Coming to a stall at forty-five degrees, a loss of nerve as you reached the steepest point of the incline. Better to get speed and gun it up the hill. But this pair was stuck mid-hill and the only choice was to back up or burn out your clutch.

The man decided to burn out the clutch, which whined in protest as they laughed. I could see the headlights, the low-digit license plate as it made the crest of the hill. Fog and the smell of the burning clutch. It was a moment I would never forget, because it ended so quickly.

11

Someone had grabbed me from behind in a choke hold. I bared my teeth, and bit into the sleeve of a heavy leather jacket, but the arms tightened against my throat. I threw my head back, hoping to hear the satisfying sound of skull making contact with nose, a pleasing celery sound that never happened.

The arms closed tighter about my neck and the world began to grow black at the edges. I aimed my boot behind me, at toes, seeking any kind of way out of the hold, something that would keep the lights from going out in front of me. I found a groin, a foot, in that order, but my attacker was immune to pain. The choke hold tightened. The Macy's boxes were pulling at my wrists as my heel finally found a crotch. It could have been a direct hit but I was out-numbered.

A bigger, darker dark shadow loomed. Like a pointed finger of doom it came closer and closer. I could hear the laughter in the open convertible as it made the top of the hill. Then the laughing stopped. I heard someone yell and all was dark. The rough feel of concrete on my cheek was my last conscious memory. Someone had picked up the sidewalk and thrown it at me.

12

Chapter Two
Iambic Pentameter

The next thing I knew Frances' dress was twisting above me from a tree top. It shimmied in front of my eyes, as if an invisible form was squirming inside the darkly glimmering shroud. The dress danced above the sidewalk to the tempo which was crashing through my head.

My eyes scanned the sidewalk searching for the old Macy's box. Then I saw it. With its lid cockeyed but still in place, the octagonal package jauntily claimed a place on the concrete, its twisted string handle reaching for my fingers. I just caught the tail lights of the convertible with the smoking clutch, a convertible which must have interrupted my mugging. It had all been over in a couple of seconds.

My fingers crawled along the pavement, found the rough surface of the handle, grasped and pulled. The box came towards me, bumping along cracked concrete and Bermuda grass. It became mine, I cradled it in my arms. Automatically, I reached for the back of my head. A large swollen lump of pain lived there.

I saw the arms of my attacker and remembered my moves. I would have heard them if it hadn't had been for the convertible. Then I could have turned, gone for the eyes. Fighting dirty didn't make me squeamish anymore. I could have taken him. But I couldn't have taken two. Your average mugging? I checked for my wallet and found it. They hadn't gone to that much trouble to steal a dress. Whoever it was had wanted Howard Blooming's final papers.

13

Or not. I knew that there was a gang working the Castro and this was their MO. They mug women on the street and lately the robbers have been getting more violent.

I found my car, started the engine and focused on the street, trying to get my night vision in order. I pulled down the window and took a deep breath of the comfortable, homey scent of Northern California. Eucalyptus and exhaust.

A big truck, lined with plywood and filled with bottles and cans, followed me home. There would be a parade tonight in our neighborhood. It was garbage night and people would be coming by to pick through the refuse for anything of value. Women with and without children, old men, young men, people in and out of wheelchairs, would work quietly and quickly through the night. They rarely spoke to one another. The rhythm of jostling glass bottles in shopping carts maneuvering over cracked sidewalks, the rustle of the five gallon garbage bags filled with Budweiser, Coors and Coca-Cola cans had become the city's late-night symphony. Tonight the sound of bottles and carts added a counterpoint to the throbbing that was emanating from the lump in the back of my head.

I pulled up to our duplex, a flat-faced Victorian Italianate, the working class cousin to Howard and David's Queen Anne. I heaved the car door open with the two boxes on my lap. I crawled off the vinyl seat into the gutter like I was a hundred years old. My hand was finding the back of my head, and doing things that was making my headache much worse, when a face emerged out of the darkness.

There were times when I didn't want to see my house partner and upstairs neighbor, Laura Deleuse. This was one of them. She sucked on a cigarette and eyed me. 'You don't look so good, Emma.'

'No, really?'

Laura was a cop and I was a legal investigator; it didn't leave us with much to say. But we'd knocked back a few beers together when we were in the mood to tell the world to go to hell. Tonight it wasn't the world that Laura wanted to go to hell. It was me. Laura squinted through the smoke of her cigarette and said nothing.

'What's with you, Laura?'

No answer.

Then, 'You don't know?'

'I'm too tired to guess. I'm just trying to get dressed for my fucking date, Laura,' I tried to move past her with the boxes in my hands.

'Then you'd better wash your hair. Your neck is bleeding.' Laura waved the orange coal of her cigarette at me, then turned her back and trudged up the front stairs, one step after the other like each leg had to make a separate decision. Each leg deciding to carry that tired torso of Sergeant Laura Deleuse, of the San Francisco Police Department, to bed. Civil servants, so busy serving and protecting. It was almost enough to make me cry. 'I don't care what you do, Emma.' She said at the top of the stairs. I could tell I was going to hear what the problem was. Soon. 'I just wish you wouldn't do it in *my* backyard.' She closed the door firmly and chained, bolted and deadlocked it.

Okay, okay. So *that's* what it was about. *The garden.* Laura was pissed about the garden. I ran my hand over my hair and down the nape of my neck. There was a small spot which was sticky with blood. Thanks for the warning, Laura.

Frances and I had come into the market when prices were inflated and interest rates high. We'd bought in with Laura Deleuse, who had some cash and needed a tax break. Frances had met her in an emergency room, while Frances was suturing a bullet hole in some crack war soldier that Laura had scraped up off the street.

She and Laura had exchanged war stories and whined about their mutual need for a tax shelter while Frances stitched and sutured. Laura was looking, like Frances, for property. But cops, and socially minded lesbian doctors can't often afford San Francisco real estate, which was as costly per square foot as Manhattan's.

15

Frances started looking and called Laura when she found something. It was right in the colorful (read 'high crime' to Laura Deleuse) lower Mission neighborhood. Laura didn't partake of the pleasures of the fresh-squeezed juices, the tostadas, the sight of *piñatas* for children's parties swinging from every bodega awning. The house was the right price, the right size and the right color.

I remembered the day we all pulled up to the residence, in a quiet Mission street, lined with bottle brush trees, and, different as we were, we knew the place was for us. I loved the house, its front painted the color of blue hydrangeas, its features iced with white scrolling. A living room was made bigger by knocking a wall through to the dining room. The back door to the garden was already ramped. A huge wardrobe was converted into a tiny office for Frances. We filled a guest room with travel souvenirs. Our two cats, Fluffy and Friend, had a cat door to go in and out of at will.

Laura didn't want any pets. She just wanted a view, the deck and, as far as we could tell, she was over wanting any kind of partner other than the one that rode in her squad car. In terms of San Francisco real estate, we could be running a three legged race for life. We lived with our differences, in the same building, with the same mortgage. Odd tenants who didn't socialize too much.

The fog hadn't penetrated into the Mission yet. I could still see stars in the sky, above the warm lights which lit up our apartment. The sound of the bottle people with their carts had receded into the distance. I opened the door and said hello to Fluffy who was too busy grooming to greet me properly. Frances was busy in her office.

'Hi honey, where've you been?' she called from her office, her voice distracted.

'I had to run an errand. For Willie. I want to see you in this dress, honey, I think it will look great.' I went into the bathroom and wiped the spot of blood off my neck. I shook my head, trying to get the taste of the sleeve of that leather jacket out of my mouth, the horrible taste of old leather, salty with sweat and reeking of aggression. I looked myself over carefully in the mirror. I didn't think there was any way Frances would notice I'd been mugged, and I wouldn't tell her, I decided. It was no reason to spoil the evening. I emerged from the bathroom and found Frances standing at the kitchen table, running her hands over the Formica surface.

Frances was thirty-two years old, five foot seven, with a slight, slim figure. She had caramel-colored hair, fine as silk, that could stand straight up with the right static conditions. More usually it fell to her small, round shoulders. A generous but determined mouth complimented her strong, pointed chin. Frances dressed in creams and beiges these days and tended to be very busy. I reached out for her lady's hips. This dress was just the ticket for Frances' lovely, compact body. I picked up the dress box from Macy's. It had been a long time since I had given Frances a present.

Frances' fingers lifted off the lid and searched through the tissue paper. The sequined material winked and glittered. Frances gasped, drawing out the gown and holding it up to the light. It shimmered and shimmied as she pressed it against her breasts and gathered it in at the waist. A perfect fit. I looked at Frances' face. She loved the dress, I could see it. But there was also something else. She was smiling, but biting her lip. 'I have to tell you something hard, honey.'

If it wasn't something major I would have felt her hands on my shoulders, her lips on my neck. I just heard silence. That was a bad sign. My imagination started to generate a host of possibilities.

'What is it?' I kept my voice even.

'I was just called by the President of the Board of the Seattle Women's Health Clinic,' Frances looked up. Her eyes were dancing, she was flushed with excitement. 'The largest women's clinic in Seattle is going to be the target of a major right-wing demonstration tomorrow. The fundamentalists are demonstrating against abortion, and – ' she took a deep breath, 'They've threatened the lives of local physicians, in print. Last night, Emma, last night, one of the physicians came home to find his house burned to the ground. His family just escaped, Emma. I have to be there – '

'Will you have some personal security? What's the story with the police?'

'The police aren't providing protection worth shit. And, Emma, there are fifty lesbian physicians whose lives have been threatened because of the reproductive services – '

'Reproductive services,' I echoed.

'Artificial insemination Emma! – the new family that the fundamentalist right doesn't think has any right to be a family.'

'Frances, it sounds like a really dangerous situation,' I said quietly. 'Why don't you let me go with you? I know the profiles, I can scan crowds – ' I stopped.

Frances looked down and checked to make sure all her fingernails were there. 'Their keynote speaker canceled,' she said quietly.

So that was it. Their keynote speaker had canceled. *Ipso facto* Frances was now their keynote speaker.

'Let me go with you – '

'Emma, you have to go to the Gala.'

I looked down at Howard Blooming's journals. It was time to be noble and brave. Frances would do her job and I would do mine.

An army of lovers could not fail. 'You'll have to make it up to me. How long do we have before your plane takes off?' But Frances was pouring coffee into a promotional car cup that had been dropped off by a pharmaceutical salesman at the clinic where she worked. '*Tetonydril*,' the words on the cup read. '*For Chlamydia and other vaginal infections.*'

'It gets worse,' Frances smiled slightly.

'What?'

'I forgot to rent your tuxedo.'

We both looked at the black sequined dress now draped over a kitchen chair. Just a slip of a thing, a tiny tube of tinsel it was. And there truly was not another fucking piece of evening wear in the house.

'I want to see you in that dress!' Frances' hazel eyes were dancing.

What was she, joking? I stared at Frances in horror. Then she laughed out loud as I pulled the garment towards me and pressed it against my chest. Whatever would I do with it? I looked into Frances' eyes again and knew. I stripped down to my bra and boxers, and viewed the dress with trepidation. Then, as if I were wrestling with a boa constrictor, the dress eating me up alive, I pulled the taut elastic material up over knees, thighs, buttocks, waist and breasts. Frances was laughing harder, crossing her legs.

The dress fit my body like a glove. Too bad I wasn't a hand. Frances was laughing so hard she almost choked, spilling coffee out of her *Chlamydia* mug.

My extra five inches of height over Frances put the hemline just on the decent side of venus, that is, *mons* venus; I looked like a working girl with hairy legs and no haircut. The material gathered by the cleft between my breasts, the scales making a soft swishing sound as they brushed against each other, like a whispered message from my *décolleté*. And then Frances wasn't laughing anymore.

'Emma, you look *gorgeous*! I want you in sequins all the time!' Frances was on her feet, kissing me hard and fast. Her swift tongue found its way between my lips, surprising me as usual, her hands roamed over my flesh, deciphering my ribs. It took less than that to make me wet.

'Hey!'

Frances had disappeared into her office again, saying 'I have to get my papers together.' And before I had time to catch my breath she had changed the subject. 'Did you read the *Bay Times* on the Archive architectural controversy?'

'Humph.' I scratched at a sequin which was digging a hole under my arm and found the paper with the cover featuring Executive Director of the Archive, Tracy Port, and Senatorial hopeful, Renquist Falkenberg, jogging in the Japanese Tea Garden, startling any number of tourists. Renquist was huffing and puffing, trying to slim down, and Tracy, as usual, looked straight ahead.

I leafed through the paper. Through some advertisements selling condos in the Victoria Mews housing complex. Wasn't that where Tracy Port lived?

I had read a police report about an unlucky occupant at Victoria Mews just last week. He'd discovered a burglary taking place at his apartment in the upscale condo development. It was what the cops call a 'hot prowl'. The burglar had a gun and had got scared. And then he became a murderer. They wouldn't mention that in the condo ads, of course.

There was mention of foolproof new security systems in the building. But no systems were foolproof, I thought as I turned to the letter section. Laura Deleuse wanted to get a security system for our house. Maybe it wasn't a bad idea.

I read a brief but glowing review of Helen Thomas' latest mystery novel, which promised that 'Luminous strokes of terror would keep the reader turning the pages until the end.' The review also mentioned that Helen would be the keynote speaker at the Archive Gala Dinner. Well, that, at least, was something to look forward to.

Then I found the letters section. Under the twenty-eight point bold cap, 'ARCHIVE CONTROVERSY CONTINUES' heading letters varying from outrage to adulation had been published about the latest community project.

There was no question that everyone thought the Archive a valuable resource and a fitting tribute to the man who had stood up against homophobia and given his life for it. But not everyone was a fan of the sheer camp and excess of it. A huge marble edifice, styled after a Greek temple, the Archive had been variously described as an eyesore and an architectural achievement, a blight and a blessing.

The Lesbian Revengers had accused the designers and Board of Directors of choosing a style that was overtly and completely male. Indeed it was hard not to see massive erect penises in the phalanx of pillars. The Board of Directors had assured the Revengers that an image of Sappho would float along the exterior frieze over the doorway. But the expense and scale of the project and the way it might be administrated continued to give pause to many.

The libertarians among us thought our history shouldn't be in the hands of the government; they thought that the papers of the lesbian and gay community should be held by a community non-profit group. What if our history was destroyed by some evil reactionary turn of political climate? The Magnus Hirschfeld's library in the Institute for Sex Research had been destroyed in Berlin in 1933 by the Nazis. Valuable papers lost to history for ever! Twelve thousand books and 35,000 photographs! It *could* happen here!

On the other hand, the civil servants, the lesbian and gay librarians, thought that all the decisions were coming from the private funders and that money was buying policy. A policy that the Archive Board of Directors was taking a very long time to come up with.

The Board had been accused of being overly concerned with the physical plant which would house the facility. The emphasis on decor made a lot of historians nervous. The final insult was an elaborate, expensive mural commissioned by the Board, to grace the ceiling of the Archive. The artist, Larry Boznian, was not only a virtual unknown in the community, he lived in New York and he was *British*. The West Coast still quivered with cultural defensiveness in the shadow of the elite East and not without good reason. San Francisco painters, so frequently passed over by local arts commissions, vented their fury in letters to the editor in the local lesbian and gay press. The rumored commission was guestimated at over 300,000 dollars! And now we had to pay $200 for the Gala Dinner ticket. Two hundred dollars to eat rubber chicken.

But as the Archive would be such an excellent investigative tool, I coughed up the dough as did several of my friends. It seemed that everybody loved libraries and archives. And everybody loved the idea of having our own.

Meanwhile, I had my own task at hand. The faded floral paper on the box from Macy's might hold a crucial part of history and it would soon be sealed away for many years. But then my thoughts were interrupted by a slim projectile whizzing out of Frances' office. Pantyhose. I opened the package and pulled out the filmy gauze.

I gathered the toe and thrust my foot in and pulled the sheer material over my legs; black hairs flattened into a hairy cross hatch pattern. There was no time or motivation to do anything about that. I stood up, pulling the elastic waistband as high as I could. I knew that there were women who could function wearing elastic hosiery every day. I wasn't one of them.

I hopped with the odd step that the low crotch gave me, over to the tool cupboard. Inside a box full of screws and staples was a roll of silver duct tape. I hopped back to the kitchen table and worked at pulling the crotch of the panty higher as I surveyed the box. The lid rested uneasily on it, the corners splayed out, the paper cracking along the edges. That bead, or button was still rolling around in there. I picked up the duct tape.

My fingernails picked at the edge of the tape and pried it loose. With a tug and a squeal the tape parted from the roll. I held it over the box. It was very sticky. Once it landed on the faded flowery paper, it would never come loose. Big secrets. Big deal. I laid the tape across the top of the box where it clung to the old paper. I ran my fingers over the material, paying particular attention to the juncture between box and lid. Around and around until the duct tape was completely used up. Howard's journals were mummified. Mission accomplished. I had won out over my own curiosity.

Despite Frances' approval of my costume, there was no way I was going to be bound by pantyhose and sequins all night. I was working.

I got out my black canvas bag which had been water-proofed inside. I slipped my lightweight cotton black pants into it. A pair of tennis shoes, a decade old, the soles worn slick and treadless. A tight-fitting black turtleneck which could be rolled up to my eyes. And for good measure I added a high intensity flashlight; and a tiny kit featuring several sizes of screwdrivers with various type heads.

There were tools that I'd rather Laura Deleuse did not know of. A set of skeleton keys which could get me in just about anywhere and a slim jim which could open almost all car doors except a Ford Taurus. No one could break into a Ford Taurus.

I put my hand up to the bump on my head. I added a can of Mace and a pair of brass numchucks on a chain into the bag. I opened it up as wide as it could go, resting Howard Blooming's box carefully on the clothes and cat burglar tools. The zipper just closed over the many items.

'C'mon honey, we gotta go,' Frances emerged from the bedroom, her hair, fresh from the brush, making a static halo around her head. I wanted nothing more than to ruin her lipstick.

And I did. Frances may have changed styles, but her kiss was still the same, like waves of iambic pentameter, *this* and then *this* and then . . .

'By the way,' Frances pulled back. 'I have something for you to bring to the Gala tonight. A donation for the Archive.'

Just what I needed. Something else to keep track of.

'Tracy called me tonight and said she wanted me to donate my original lab notes on *Lesbo-Parthenogenesis*.'

Lesbo-Parthenogenesis – the combining of two ovums to create a female child – was in reality far, far, off. But Frances had had some limited success with female parthenogenesis in frogs. There were some exciting breakthroughs, but she had always kept her experiments relatively quiet; only parts of the lesbian community were aware of this work.

'I'm still working out the terms of access with her,'

Frances went on, 'the Board is taking for ever to come up with a policy.'

'Sure, give them to me.' Frances handed over a thin pile of notebooks. Inside would be tiny grids and perfect little printed notes. I tucked the notes carefully under my arm. 'What time does your plane leave?'

'About eight thirty.' She turned her back to pull the car keys off a hook on the wall. 'By the way, Laura said that the garden is looking a little weedy.' Ah, yes. The garden. Laura often relayed her coded messages through Frances when the marijuana crop I was raising for the Hemp For Health movement was getting a little too obvious for her professional comfort.

'Yeah, she growled at me on the stairs. Well, sweetheart, rubber chicken time!' I could avoid unpleasant topics just as easily as Frances could. I looked again at my lover's face and features. Busy. Brilliant. Diligent. Driven and dedicated. I wanted to kiss her again, to suck the magenta color off the precious pillows that were her lips, to slide my tongue between her teeth, to kiss her and make her fly. Frances, however, was in a hurry. She picked up her coffee cup for her last hit of caffeine. '*Tetonydril. For Chlamydia and other vaginal infections.*' We walked down to the car in silence, each carrying our various burdens.

'Are you okay?' Frances was asking as we pulled up to the curb.

'Yes,' I lied, looking the crowd over with deepening dismay. There was an air of liberal guilt, a disturbing wind that would determine the tone of the evening. The kind of event that cost two hundred dollars drew the kind of people that could pay for it. All the women would be wearing lipstick. None of the men would be wearing dresses. I sighed, the upper middle class lesbians and gays, as always, were gender predictable.

'What fresh hell is this?' I muttered, looking up at the finished building, remembering the angry letters from lesbians in the *Bay Times*, complaining about the architecture. Each Ionic pillar, indeed, looked like a cross section of a penis and each one was lit up in a different color of the rainbow. I was still holding with one hand the black canvas bag which contained the sticky ball of tape that was Howard Blooming's final papers, Frances' original lab notes on *Lesbo-Parthenogenesis* with the other.

'Well, this is it, babe,' I looked into those starburst hazel eyes, the carefully styled pageboy, the way her fingertips grazed the bumps along the steering wheel. 'I'm really sorry I can't be here.'

'Yeah,' I said, managing a smile and looking at the crowd which tripped up the stairs in evening clothes.

'I've got to be going.' Frances slid her arms around me and pulled me close. 'I love you, Emma.'

'What time does your plane get in? Did you leave a phone number?'

'In case of emergency,' she said, an unstated warning. She would be in professional mode. She wouldn't want me to call.

I leaned forward slowly and planted a long kiss on her lipsticked lips, then clambered out of the car. The bulky canvas bag seemed to have a life of its own, as it bounced on my hip. The elasticized minidress clung uncomfortably to my body and crawled embarrassingly skywards as I struggled to get my legs out, every inch of thigh exposed. Fate found for me the perfect witness of this humiliation.

'Oh, hi Tracy.' I clung to my bag and papers, praying I wouldn't drop anything, trying to stand up straight. The last thing I wanted to do was bend over in front of Tracy Port in this dress. My gaze traveled up Tracy's stone calves, those marvelous hamstrings and sturdy knees. What would Tracy be wearing to an event like this?

What else? *Frances' dress*. She wore it much better than I did and from the look on her face we both knew it.

Tracy turned around, looking me up and down, her eyes noting the unshaved legs, the inappropriate shoes, the barely decent way the dress clung to my fuller, taller, figure. 'Emma, you're a picture!' she said, and then she turned around to show me how it should be done.

She bent down to say hello to Frances. The dress didn't ride up, it just seemed to hug the pair of pillows that were Tracy's buttocks and make her calves pull tighter above her slim ankles. My sequins were becoming a hairshirt now as Frances' attention glided over the slinky surface of the Executive Director of the Archive. Frances didn't seem in such a hurry to make the airport anymore.

'Well, well, Tracy, this is your big night,' she burbled. 'Congratulations!' They exchanged air kisses through the open car window.

'My God, Tracy, you're wearing my dress,' Frances was saying. 'I had forgotten to pick up Emma's tux – ' Tracy turned around momentarily to look at me again. They chuckled.

'So *that's* what happened! Aren't you coming tonight?'

'I'm so *sorry* I can't be here – '

I moved my bulky packages around in my arms and coughed. The corners of the box were biting into my side. The *Lesbo-Parthenogenesis* notes picked up a breeze and ruffled themselves like feathers underneath my arm. I looked over the crowd and thought about the headache that was going to accompany me tonight. I needed to let go of the packages. I needed to let go of Frances.

'Bye Frances,' I called out. She looked over Tracy's shoulder at me and smiled. I set off to find the office of Allen Boone.

Chapter Three

Genre

Vaults keep the secrets which can be ravaged in the present. I couldn't help but feel like Howard Carter, exhuming things better left buried, burying things which might be better off revealed. The Archive would house it all at the discretion of donors who would hand over their letters, journals, photos, manuscripts and other document-ation of lesbian and gay lives. The shifting tides of attitudes, the moments of danger, passion, friendship, and love all guarded in a big vault at the end of the long hallway.

I stood behind a double combination locked fireproof door labeled 'STAFF ONLY' and listened to voices. Whoever the staff were they didn't sound happy.

A door at the end of the hallway opened and closed. I looked up and saw a small man in his late forties, mopping his brow with a handkerchief. His pleated shirt was wrig-gling free of a pink cummerbund at his waist.

The voices behind the door were mean and exasperated, seeming to echo through the hallway. The man came closer and saw me. 'Oh!' An instant broad grin split his face. He was bald, possibly shaved, and had a well-developed torso carried on short legs. Underneath heavy eyebrows, blue eyes lit up as he watched me pull the flowered box covered with duct tape from the bag in my hand. 'You must be Emma Victor?'

'That's right.' I shook the warm, dry hand of the assistant curator of the Lesbian and Gay Memorial Archive. Dry palms, perfect for touching paper. 'I believe you're expecting this.' I held out the box. Allen's eyes gleamed. 'The final journals and papers of Howard Blooming,' he beamed. 'To have them here in our Archive!' He took the box into his arms and gazed at it lovingly.

'Shouldn't we lock them in the vault or something?'

Angry voices drifted out from behind the door.

'Actually, the vault isn't completely finished,' he smiled. 'In fact, a great deal of it is hardly finished at all! We're still trying to get donations – '

The voices hit an especially high note.

'A bit of a misunderstanding,' he murmured.

'I'd like to get these locked up in the vault – '

'The vault, no, no, no! You don't understand. It's not even finished – '

'But I have to secure a place for the papers.'

'Well, we do have a safe. An old safe that one of the gay bankers gave us. All their money is on computer now. I suppose you could – '

'Yes, why don't I.' Not wanting to waste any more time, I put my hand on the door with the combination lock. The voices behind it seemed to rise in response.

'This door isn't engaged from the outside, yet. Sorry! You can go in through my office – my temporary office.' I stepped into a dark, fetid room. It took a while for my eyes to get used to the dim light. I could see that there were books and papers everywhere. Eventually I made out old suitcases with molding leather straps piled high on top of each other and topped with a row of rotting briefcases. All over the walls were pictures with and without frames.

'I haven't really been able to unpack yet,' he apologized. 'They gave me an office without windows, you see – '

'You've got a lot of stuff here – '. Stacks of LPs and 78s topped with flowered biscuit tins caught my attention. The LPs had been carefully wrapped in plastic and sealed with cellophane tape.

'I know, it doesn't look like there is a system, but there is, believe me.'

I picked up a napkin from the Paper Doll Café, carefully tucked inside a pink cocktail menu. Someone had noted the date on the back in light pencil. Nineteen fifty-four.

'There,' Allen pushed me gently out of his office and towards what I supposed was the soon-to-be-completed vault.

Vaults are not what people expect them to be. A long cement block structure, often a room within a room, humidity controlled and monitored. I could see that the basement of the Archive had been sectioned off to house different kinds of items. 'FILM,' I read over one door, but the door was open and nothing was inside. Concrete walls stretched indefinitely into the basement of the Archive. Metal shelving was still being constructed. Rows of acid-free boxes stood ready to receive documents.

A reception area was laid out behind a pair of double doors. There was a desk with a series of cubbyholes behind it where researchers would check in their bags and a reading table with two rows of straightbacked chairs. A receptionist with eagle eyes and a closed circuit camera would monitor the handling of materials. But right now, nothing was ready except the safe.

It was a big antique, claiming a central area of the floor. If nothing else, it was a marvelous decoration. A foot thick steel door, studded with brass bolts, was opened on greased hinges to show off glittering rows of numbered safety deposit boxes. Out of the lock on each box hung two finely wrought keys.

Howard's journals would fit into one of the larger boxes. But there was no way I could get to it without interrupting the heated discussion taking place in the cold basement. 'A receipt. I just want a receipt for my manuscripts –' a voice I recognized was saying. It belonged to Helen Thomas, keynote speaker at the dinner. The prolific mystery writer had her hands on hips. A black silk shirtwaist dress accented her small waist, bronze piping setting off a dramatic flange of a collar which framed a swan like neck. The centre-piece of her dark décolleté was her famous filigreed amulet. The amber amulet had been a gift from her patron, poet Berniece Able. There was a history behind that amulet. A history Helen very effectively used.

The amulet was purported to have cyanide in it. Allegedly belonging to Rasputin, the lover of the Czarina of Russia, it was supposed to have reached the possession of a peasant in Byelorussia after the revolution. And that peasant was an ancestor of Berniece Able. The amulet was passed down matrilineally through the family and gained a reputation for keeping problem husbands in line. When Berniece wanted a way to help her favorite young author she gave Helen the family heirloom, told her to have it appraised, then sell it and keep the money.

Helen, instead, had it appraised and publicized. She fictionalized the story of the amulet in her book *Grand-mother's Poison* and her career took off. Telling stories had always been Helen's best asset. And the amulet, worth perhaps a million dollars, stayed always around her neck, glowing with a sharp yellow glint against her chest. Helen wore it with a cunning sense of style.

Now, however, Helen was not looking stylish. Her face was turning purple and her body was twisted with fury. A towering column of white manuscript boxes balanced precariously on the foot of a hand truck next to her.

I saw the low spark of black sequins in the half-darkness. It could have only been Tracy Port. I moved back towards the chaotic darkness of Allen's office.

Tracy was sighing dramatically. 'Look Helen, I'm short of time here. I interrupted an important conversation with someone to help you bring your scripts in the Archive, but I had no idea – *no idea* – that you meant all this!'

I looked at the manuscript boxes. How many pages were there? I figured that Helen had written twenty-seven books.

In a pile that size there must be seven drafts of each book. The forests must have groaned when Helen started writing.

'We can't possibly take all this into the Archive, Helen. Think of the hours of microfilming – the volunteer corps, hunched over the photographic machines – '

'You mean you don't *want* my manuscripts?' Helen's voice was low and dull, dull like a knife. Her petticoats seemed to grow in volume under the black tulle.

'Perhaps we could consider the *award-winning* ones? The first and last drafts of each?'

Helen narrowed her eyes. 'They've *all* won awards Tracy! This body of work charts the development of twenty-seven plots – which chronicles a parallel development of a new way of thinking about suspense – about *justice*! I have *struggled* – and been *acknowledged*.'

But Tracy had 1500 guests to acknowledge. 'I have no time to argue, Helen. Perhaps if you didn't change your *plots* so *often*.' Tracy's voice had an edge of sarcasm, an edge she couldn't control.

'Are you rejecting my manuscripts, Tracy?'

'That's exactly what I'm doing Helen. You write pot-boilers. It's made you rich. But they're hardly artifactually significant!'

'If you have such contempt for my work, then why did you ask me to be the keynote speaker at your event?' The question hung in the air. It didn't need an answer. 'It's because I'm black, that's why you needed me here, isn't it?' Helen gritted her teeth. 'All those flattering phone calls!' I could see the tendons in Helen's neck standing out. 'You realize I passed up being on the panel at the BlackOUT Film Festival to add a little color to your podium?'

The BlackOUT Film Festival. No wonder Helen was pissed. I hoped she wouldn't go ballistic.

'Oh, now Helen, don't you think you're being just a little paranoid? Why don't you go back to your table? Back to your dear, darling, Lee? Maybe if you're really sweet she'll give you another convertible. In the meantime, I'll find a way of disposing of these.' She punctuated her suggestion with a dismissive flick of her toe at the scripts.

'Lee?' Helen murmured. The word began with a surprised whisper and ended in a horrible, heart-breaking certainty.

'Think about it, Helen. You'll never know what really happened on that boat.' And with that Tracy turned and strode away quickly into the back of the basement, on her taut little legs.

Helen Thomas clutched the amulet around her neck and said something to herself. I saw her struggle with bad thoughts and I thought I saw her win. But she walked away quickly after Tracy Port, towards what I guessed must be the stairs from the basement up to the Gala Dinner.

When I turned around I found I was not alone. Allen Boone was behind me in the darkness staring intently at the box in my hand as if he could see through it and read all that was inside.

'Just a misunderstanding,' he said, quickly, 'It's really the Board's fault. The time they take to come up with policy decisions! We *still* don't have acceptance guidelines. They're so inept it is practically impossible for us to do our jobs!' Allen was talking a mile a minute as he eyed the box that held Howard Blooming's journals.

'Shall we put these in the safe now?' I asked.

'Oh Emma,' Allen gazed up at me, reluctantly. 'What were David's instructions exactly?'

'Sealed,' I said. 'Sealed for sixty years.'

'Oh.' Allen's face fell by degrees. 'Sixty years,' he breathed. I could almost heart him counting. We'd all be dead in sixty years. Then Allen's face went from white to pink. A strange tapping, like four canes rapping, was coming towards us.

Tap, tap, tap, tap, scrape. It was a familiar sound, and the figure which accompanied it, the person who drove the walker through Allen's office was none other than Pulitzer Prize-winning poet Berniece Able.

Already she was shouting. 'What in hell do I have to do

to get into this totally inaccessible shit hole?' I could see Berniece's large ivory teeth, yellow, with thin black stripes down the center of them, the pallid pouches of her cheeks filling with air as she bore down upon us. Berniece had a hard sharp gaze, encased in rubbery features. A large canvas bag hung off of each fleshy shoulder. 'And there has been *no one* to brief me!'

Allen was so busy apologizing to Berniece Able and helping her with her load that he had almost forgotten about Howard Blooming's journals. I saw his hands tremble as he took the cloth sacks from Berniece.

'Berniece, I'm so sorry – '

'Well, Allen, you've been hounding me for my scrapbooks for years. Years. So here they are.' She smiled suddenly, her eyes becoming little gleaming crescents.

'Berniece,' Allen was clearly moved. He leaned over the railing of her walker to give her a big hug. 'It's been a long time since I was shown to the back door,' Berniece fondly admonished him.

'Oh, Berniece, the scrapbooks!' Allen could hardly contain himself. He pulled out one of the older photo albums and dropped immediately to the floor. Sitting cross-legged, he fingered the soft black paper. I moved closer and squinted at the yellowed prints that Allen was scanning so closely. 'Yes, yes,' Allen breathed, 'Here's Djuna Barnes.'

'I thought she was a recluse.' I said.

Berniece Able looked up at me for the first time. She let go of her walker with one hand to wave away a white strand of hair. She squinted her watery blue eyes, the little round mouth with the sagging lower lip pulling together in some negative decision. 'You're a gossip queen, Allen,' Berniece said. 'Put the books down before the acid in your skin eats away all the faces of my former friends.'

'Thank you, Berniece,' Allen bowed slightly. 'We are so very grateful I can't tell you, this kind of acquisition is exactly . . .'

'Stop bowing and scraping. I'm glad to get rid of them.

What a ghost list! All my friends are dead now. But, I suppose I have Lee and Helen. I can't really complain.'

Ah, yes, didn't I remember that Berniece Able had been responsible for the match between Lee Turgo, her neighbor and chiropractor for years, and Helen Thomas? Lee Turgo had Rolfed Berniece Able into a standing position when the elderly poet was in deep pain, permanently hunched over, it seemed. Lee had continued to care for the aging laureate and Berniece Able had become very attached to the young healer.

In between poems Berniece used to look out of her kitchen window and see Lee getting led around by anything femme that flopped, including a lot of gold diggers. Berniece Able had decided to make it her personal mission to match Lee Turgo with someone suitable.

Helen Thomas, Berniece's old student, filled the bill. Berniece worked behind the scenes to get the two together and watched with pleasure as they consolidated their lives next door to her. A new kind of extended family, the three women took turns taking care of each other with a combination of publishing advice, spinal adjustments, ready cash and old recipes.

'Here!' Berniece hauled out a photobook from the seventies. The cover was upholstered with silk and embroidered with bright orange flowers. 'Helen made the cover for me, when she was a student.' Berniece still sounded proud. I imagined Helen, as a college student, spending hours over this sentimental handy-work, an offering to a teacher in a history of handicraft offerings from female students to female teachers. Perfect for the Archive.

'Did she sign it?' Allen was asking as Berniece handed the precious book over to Allen and watched him open it.

'Oh no!' Allen whispered.

'What?' Berniece demanded.

'Nothing, Berniece, nothing.'

I noticed that the photos had been trapped between

gummed cellophane pages and cardboard. 'This gummed adhesive, the images – ' Allen muttered under his breath.

'Look, there's that vampire Tracy Port.' Berniece poked a finger at a younger Tracy Port with long, hippy girl hair. Her legs, skinny before the fitness craze, were crossed under an Indian bedspread miniskirt.

'Please, Berniece, she's my boss.'

'I'm eighty. I'll say what I like!' Berniece shrugged her shoulders. 'Get off the floor, man!' she barked at Allen. 'And stop whining about glue! I wasn't recording history when I pasted those in, I was having an affair!'

'Yes, of course, sorry, Berniece.'

'Take the scrapbooks and do what you will.' Berniece picked up her walker and pounded all four feet upon the floor in unison. Sometimes I wondered if she needed the walker at all. 'And you, young lady,' Berniece aimed her sights at me sternly. 'Don't assume every biography you read is true. There's a lot of trumped up, closeted garbage out there masquerading as history. That's what this Archive is for – '

Just then Allen came up with the wonderful idea that Berniece and I should both present the historic acquisitions during the Gala Dinner. 'It's just going to make the evening. To let everyone know the kind of material we're getting.' He beamed. 'What a *show*!' He moved Berniece towards his office door.

'I really think Howard's journals should be in the safe – ' I protested.

'Too late!' Allen said, ushering us out of the office and locking the door behind him. I leaned with a groan against the double combination lock door in the corridor. The sequined dress was strangling my body, and the box covered with sticky tape seemed to cling to me. It was beginning to feel impossible to get rid of.

Chapter Four

Appetizers

Above ground, the cavernous hall was filled with tables covered in snowy white cloths and laden with heavy-handled silverware. Odd centerpieces poked up from tables. Birds of paradise stuck into cement blocks at a steep angle and, draped with ivy, reminded me of the unfinished vault below.

I looked up at the ceiling. The Mid-Atlantic import had done a dramatic job. Above us stretched the twisting torsos of muscle-laden figures flying across the plastered heaven. Multiracial bodies in fresco showed off their pecs and abs as they seemingly threw books to the heavens.

A huge, diaphanously clad female, her dark maroon breasts just visible underneath an Isadora Duncan nightie, her arms rippling with biceps, attempted to touch the out-stretched hand of an effete gay male poet. God as a massive black lesbian. Larry Boznian's idea of camp.

So was the crowd of seraphim which featured faces of local celebrities. I'd heard that for the price of five hundred bucks, you could get yourself a place on the ceiling for eternity. Some donors had opted for hell, where a gaggle of leather-clad literati happily roasted hot dogs over burning hellfire and brimstone.

'Hey Victor!' That sounded like good news. I spun around to see Rose Baynetta coming straight at me in her wheel-chair. Rose was my friend, and sometime colleague who ran a private security agency.

Her curly blond hair formed a silvery frame around a face that was always brown, the result of many freckles crammed close together. Her skin contrasted greatly with her violet eyes. Rose had worked hard, worried harder and charged handsomely for her services, providing surveillance, bodyguards, and state-of-the-art techno-sleuthing.

Rose paid her operatives well, and I'd had occasion to use several of the simian types Rose employed. Rose herself had been visiting the gym a lot lately. She showed off her arms in a sleeveless silk T-shirt and I noticed a recent 'Rose' tattoo. Few people knew that her entire back was wallpapered. A lot of people only saw that Rose was paralyzed from the waist down.

'Glad to see someone in drag here, Emma,' Rose snorted staring at my dress. 'See! The only lipstick is on lesbians. No gender bending here. Go figure! What is lesbian and gay life about? As if establishing your sexual identity is the end of the journey. What happened, your dress shrink or something?'

'Thanks Rose.'

'We're at the same table. Allen arranged it. Now *there's* a human being! Have you met him yet, Emma?'

'Tell me about him.'

'He's an archivist. He's worked for the Lesbian and Gay Historical Society since the beginning. His clippings collection is something to leaf through. His mind is a card catalogue of all things Lesbian and Gay stretching back to the beginning of civilization! He's been sort of weekend lovers with Renquist for I don't know how long. What's that you've got there?' She indicated the canvas bag, where I'd shoved Howard's box on the way up from the vault.

'Rose, I want to talk to you. I've got something – '

But a lot of noise, a lot of political noise, interrupted us. Renquist Falkenberg, City Supe and Senatorial Hopeful, was right behind us.

'Hi there, how are you all?' The large African American

man cut a dramatic figure. I watched him carefully as he extended his hand to a vast range of people in turn.

Renquist Falkenberg had the grace and ease that only large people can have. He looked like a big whale tonight, outfitted in an oversized tux. And yet graceful, a whale in water. Political water.

He was thirty-three years old, and three hundred pounds in weight. His brain covered up with a lot of brawn. But that brain was ticking away there all the time.

The handshake would be warm; the hug would be overwhelming: Renquist had spotted me. I prepared myself.

'EMMA!'

After an almost indiscernible pause, Renquist opened his arms and enfolded me in an embrace.

Why was it that so many people enjoyed hugging Renquist, myself included?

I found myself smiling as I surfed along the rim of Renquist's big belly. The silver Mojos dangling from his neck pressed against my cheeks, leaving temporary tattoos on my face.

The Renquist hug was dispensed liberally. If you listened carefully you could almost hear the pens punching the voter's booths as he made his way through the crowd. It was an experience to be savored. You never felt like the same person after the Renquist hug. Renquist hugged at every reception, brunch and benefit. I hoped that his latest jogging efforts with Tracy would not eradicate the pleasing belly. He released me as he noticed my large canvas bag.

'What do you have there Emma?'

'A donation for the Archive.' The journals seemed suddenly heavier as Renquist scanned the bag.

'Lovely! I thought maybe it was a Generation X accessory!'

'It's Howard Blooming's final journals.'

'*What?*' the large jaw slackened and his eyes became rounded.

I opened the zipper of the canvas bag and gave him a glimpse of the box.

'Where did you get them?' he said quietly. Very quietly.

'From David Stimpson.'

'Why is all that tape wrapped – '

'Sealed for sixty years.'

There was a brief silence. 'Well, Howard always knew what he was doing, didn't he? Now, if you'll excuse me, Emma.' And Renquist drifted away.

Howard Blooming had made it clear that he wished his successor to be Falkenberg. He had chosen well. But the choice had never sat well with David. After Howard's death Falkenberg had eagerly turned Howard's political capital into filling for his campaign coffers, with liberal money from as far away as Hollywood. He helped closeted gay movie stars who wanted to assuage their guilt, to become anonymous donors to various causes, groups that fought for the civil rights of people who *had* come out. None of it made David happy.

Renquist brought the African American community into some formerly lily white organizations, the often-white groups always grateful for the diversity that Renquist's dark face brought. But Renquist brought a lot more than that. He brought sound judgement and an even hand to all disputes; he was an able deal maker who constructed win-win situations out of communication breakdown.

As I looked up, Deborah Dunton, the couples counselor, and author of the bestselling *Lesbians Who Love Too Much* approached. I shuddered as she swayed up to our table.

Deborah Dunton was twenty-nine years old, medium weight, medium height and medium intelligence. She had dishwater blond hair, a southern accent which she tried to conceal, and a master's degree in social work. She had a brow that worked overtime to look earnest and she always wore expensive Italian shoes. Frances and I had consulted with her a few times. *Her* unconscious had made us cut short our therapy.

Deborah Dunton was a very kind and understanding therapist. Until you left her. The visits to her office in a condo the size of an airplane hanger in Victoria Mews were something I would have liked to forget for ever. She hadn't done anything rotten that I could actually put my finger on. She liked to sit next to me on her couch. She gave Frances her therapeutic schedule so that Frances could call her during her free hours. She encouraged Frances to do so. Once, when Frances was out of town, Dunton called to make sure I was okay. I had been fine. Until she had called.

Dunton had the kind of movable boundaries that caused wars between countries. Between dykes it was disaster.

Her status had almost floundered during an ill-fated Olivia Cruise. She'd been in a relationship with Tracy Port. Then when Tracy had expressed some interest in one of the women-only pleasure cruises to the Bahamas, Dunton had booked tickets as a birthday surprise. She'd reserved separate rooms and hoped for the best.

Once on the boat, however, Tracy had avoided her. And she had thrown herself with enthusiasm at the cruise chiropractor and hired the smouldering Lee Turgo.

Lee had had a lot of spare time on her hands, time to pine over being continually left alone while Helen Thomas went off on one book tour after another. No one quite knew if Lee Turgo had succumbed. But they did know that Deborah Dunton had been dumped. She had been publicly humiliated as she experienced snub after snub at every bridge party and scuba diving expedition, and each time she appeared on deck.

Of course enough people who knew Deborah were there, to watch her having her heart broken. Word got out. A few columnists made snide reference to her personal life and after that, the sales of *Lesbians Who Love Too Much* had dropped. But they picked up again. It seemed that lesbians, at least some lesbians, would always love too much.

Between a nice trust fund, an assured clientele and book sales, Deborah Dunton quickly got back on her feet. After a major donation, she was elected President of the Board of the Howard Blooming Lesbian and Gay Memorial Archive. Of which Tracy Port was Executive Director. They were friends again.

'So, Emma, how're things going?' Dunton fingered shiny ebony beads which held a white silk blouse closed.

'Okay, I guess.' I had set the canvas bag firmly between my feet.

'Where's Frances tonight?' Deborah's tone was always neutral, but perky.

I searched for an answer that would require the least explanation. 'Working.'

'And how are things going with your relationship?' Dunton ventured.

'To *what*? Therapists with bad boundaries?'

'My, my, testy aren't we?' Deborah raised her thin brown eyebrows, 'It seems like you still have some leftover issues – '

I was saved by the arrival of Carla Ribera.

'Blast from the past,' Rose grunted as her ex wandered over.

'Just back from Rome!' Carla announced, her lips a fierce slash of red.

Carla Ribera was a fashion photographer who could wear the clothes as well as she could shoot them. Five foot ten, and a big woman, she had couture clothes cut to her hefty size. The result was always a success. An exquisitely cut Edwardian jacket of teal blue lay over a silk shirt with flounces at the cuff. The open neck gave Carla a kind of pirate look, perfect for the business she was in. Her black silky curls were brushed high off her forehead and trickled down the middle of her back. Carla had been a hippy, but now she was a jet setter. She looked the part. A bit severe, but breathtaking. Unfortunately, that included the pungent smoke of a Gauloise Carla was waving around the room. A small dapper man was standing behind her.

'Just back from Rome!' Carla announced again.

'Where nobody minds breathing your second-hand smoke, Carla,' Rose drawled. 'Bought a new closet for your clothes and your life yet?'

'Oh Roseanna, why don't you get an identity instead of identity politics,' Carla Ribera shot back. A small, but grim, grin passed between them. Carla had pruned Rose from her life when her fashion career had taken off.

I looked back at Carla, who blew smoke high up into the air from that large red mouth, her black curls trailing over her shoulders. How, how had this image of trendiness ever bonded with the rough and ready Rose?

Easy. Carla used to be a documentary filmmaker. During the shooting of one of Carla's films she interviewed activists who were in wheelchairs. She didn't expect to fall in love with one of her subjects. But Roseanna Baynetta, known by most of us simply as Rose, had had the face of a state fair queen and a tongue like a razor. She had been a ballet dancer before a car accident had cut short her career. The dramatic story made good film footage. And Rose's hands had given Carla a few surprises too.

Rose's father had been at the wheel when the accident occurred. The other driver had been drunk, but Rose's father had hardly been sober. After the accident he had pushed Rose away from him, sending her to boarding schools and showering her with expensive gifts. He was in the security business and worked for several large fashion houses. Rose didn't want his money or the dresses. Rose wanted his equipment.

Slowly she learned the security trade and gathered his cast-off equipment. She and Carla joined forces. Rose investigated and uncovered. Carla made documentary films from the results. They collaborated on a number of projects during their five year relationship.

But then Carla got tired. Tired of applying for grants, tired of giving benefits for her films, tired of fighting the network system in the States, tired of being cast in a minority slot. Rose introduced Carla to her father who helped her get an interview with a large fashion house in Paris. Carla's pictures stopped moving and her career took off.

Then Carla restyled her hair, her clothes and her sexuality to fit her new life. With her high class couturier and a femme top in bed, Carla Ribera jetted around the world and laid every runway model in a jet set version of '*Lesbians Who Love Too Little*'. She never made another documentary. Rose pretended, with misplaced righteousness, to despise her. Rose couldn't forgive her. Carla couldn't forgive Rose for not forgiving her. It was tiresome. And it was not over.

'She's still in love with me,' Rose confided.

'All those foreign locales and long-legged models must be just a pose,' I agreed.

'Ahem!' A spoon found a glass and everyone stopped talking.

'I would like to present to you all,' Carla bellowed formally, 'the creator of the mural which spans above us, Larry Boznian!'

The small man behind her was ushered towards us. He was about fifty, with a square patch of fur under his lip and the largest ears I had seen since the Mickey Mouse Club. He was wearing a red checked sportsjacket. Larry Boznian pressed his lips tightly together in what might pass for a smile.

'It's fabulous!' Allen cooed.

'What an accomplishment!' Renquist congratulated him.

Larry looked entirely overwhelmed by so much attention, but Carla Ribera came to the rescue. 'I want you all to welcome Larry to San Francisco. He's here with – Larry, where is Fresca?'

'She's in the *loo*,' Larry said, his voice a surprise. That clipped accent, the *loo*! I looked at the painter. He really didn't seem the creative type. Everything about him was exceedingly neat and kept up, like a well-tended garden. The little beard, bow tie, the suit with the pressed plaid pleated pants. Only his hands belied his profession.

His nails were torn from prying open paint lids, his fingertips stained with the mud color of mixed pigments. He hid his hands quickly when he saw me notice them, then reached quickly for a drink. But his fingers were pressed down by another, new hand. A hand, it seemed, that didn't want him to pick up that glass.

It was a brown hand with strong fingers. Broad fingernails, cut short, with sea-shell pink nails. Bronze buffed arms that would have made Fabio jealous.

But these biceps were covered with the silky brown hide of a woman. A woman, I saw, as my eyes traveled upwards, dressed entirely in rags. How they remained on her body was hard to tell. Most of her T-shirt had been worn away, revealing a mottled pink tank top, underneath whose deep armholes a grey athletic bra was visible.

She was tall, almost six feet, and her jeans had a hard time clinging to her two shelves of hip bone. A pair of paisley patterned jockey shorts worked their way up around her waist. The jeans were ripped in long tears down the front and back; most of the butt was worn away. White horizontal threads, like ladders, tried to keep the knees together and, with the aid of a few safety pins, managed to succeed. The jeans, so marvelously inappropriate for the occasion, and those tawny biceps, almost made me afraid to look at her face. I didn't want to be disappointed.

A large birthmark was laid like a ruby at the base of her throat. But the goddess had not stopped her perfect work with that sculpted neck.

She had a heart-shaped face, a pointed chin and broad cheekbones, a determined expression. Dark brown hair had been arranged by a rat in a large nest all over her head. Her eyes had the shape of caraway seeds and flickered constantly. She was observant.

I wondered what kinds of words would emerge from her mouth. Would she speak English? How old was she anyway? She couldn't possibly be as young as she looked.

Or she wouldn't be here. Would she? And why on earth was she here with Larry Boznian? Her eyes found mine and stayed there for a moment. There was a careful flatness in those eyes. But the only remaining empty chair was next to me. She was going to have to sit in it. I held my breath as she pulled the chair to the table.

I found myself looking at the tender juncture where her jeans struggled to cover the paisley boxer shorts of silk. The silk stretched, almost shiny, like a patterned sealskin over her pubis.

'Any closer and your face is going to be in her lap,' Rose whispered but she was watching her too, watching the way her clothes moved over rippling ribs.

'Please, can we all take our seats now,' Renquist was booming. 'Allen, Deborah, let's see, we're still missing, Helen Thomas and Lee, Lee Turgo. There's Larry, and yes, sorry, Francesca Alcazon, correct? Nice to meet you, Francesca. Here comes Tracy – '

'It's *Fresca* Alcazon.' Her voice was deep and honey-toned. She turned to me.

'And you are?'

'Emma Victor,' I held out my palm and experienced her confident, strong, handshake. She smiled into my eyes. And then the smile was gone.

'*I address my caress, my caresses to the one who blesses who blesses me –* ' It was Larry Boznian and Larry Boznian was getting drunk.

'What?' I looked over at him, bewildered.

'Gertrude Stein,' Fresca explained, her top lip tightening.

'Don't let her be modest. Fresca is author of *Language Empiricism: Gertrude Stein and the Repudiation of Syntactical Causality.*' Larry said proudly, 'which won the Modern Language – '

'Larry, please, you make it too important,' Fresca said.

'*And as noon and as there was a morning and as there was morning and more than so soon and as soon.*' Larry continued, rhapsodic.

45

Fresca rolled her eyes.

'And this is Helen Thomas.' Renquist had drawn Larry and Fresca's attention to the other side of the table where Helen Thomas had just arrived.

'The mystery novelist?' Fresca asked in a measured tone. Helen nodded.

'I've read all your books. I'm so glad to meet you.'

'Thank you,' Helen's eyes blinked slowly, long lashes grazing her cheek. 'That's always lovely to hear.'

Renquist continued the introductions. 'And here's Helen's partner, Lee Turgo.'

Ah yes, Lee Turgo, the object of the romantic competition between Helen and Tracy. I didn't get it, but women went wild over Lee Turgo.

She was in her mid-thirties, five foot nine, medium build with a big swathe of auburn hair which fell boyishly over her brow. A tall, quiet, diligent woman, she had big hands, a big heart, and big bedroom baby blue eyes. She had worked her way through naturopathy school as a masseuse, eventually becoming skilled in iridology, hydrotherapy, aromatherapy, chiropractic, chinese herbal medicine and business. They say she gave quite the treatment. I looked over at her hands, the broad palms, and the tiny, perfectly manicured white nails. Lee Turgo had long, thick fingers.

She also now had four clinics and forty employees on payroll. If you were lucky, very lucky, you could maybe get an appointment with her someday. The woman with the warm hands was usually booked, but they said you were never the same after her treatment.

'Look honey, that's you!' Berniece's scrapbook was being shown around. Helen was cooing over it, stroking Lee's neck as they hunched over the photographs. Lee Turgo put her arm around Helen's waist and peered closer, that shock of auburn hair falling into her eyes.

'Sure is.' Lee Turgo was a woman of few words and little sentimentality. She scratched the side of her neck as she viewed the pictures.

'It's that baptism, honey – '

'Yeah, I remember.'

'There you are – in bell bottom pants! And look at all the babies!'

'Babies in arms, strollers and slings. Babies nursing, bottle feeding, sleeping, crying, fussing, laughing,' Berniece mused. 'Hey, that's you, Allen!' Her finger roamed over the page. 'And Renquist!' Carla Ribera came over and bent low over the book. 'Didn't you take those pictures?' Berniece enquired.

'No, I – '

'Yes you did,' Berniece insisted. 'Come on Carla, you started out as a shutterbug just like everyone else.'

'Wait, photograph!' A twenty-nothing someone, somewhere between sprite and hag appeared with a Polaroid camera. It must have been a *she*, I thought, examining the milky white cleavage which was trying to escape a bustier that had seen better days. Then I realized I had seen her somewhere before. I stared at her tattered stockings and at the garments – at least three of them – that were once called dresses and which had been pulled helter-skelter over her head. She glittered. She was pierced and perforated in every visible spot on her body. Oh, yes! It was Gurl Jesus, waitress at Red Dora's café. And now, it seemed, gala photographer.

With her pierced eyebrow, ears, cheek and chin, Gurl glittered just like the flashbulbs she was popping at the diners at our table. She was taking photo after photo. Photos of Tracy, moving behind Helen; of Renquist hugging Fresca a second time; of Fresca pushing him away. Of Allen talking earnestly to Berniece Able, who couldn't stop turning the pages of memories in front of her, memories which she was about to give away for ever.

Flash! Flash! Tracy managed a grin just as the bulb went off. Then she stood up. 'I have to start this fucking ceremony before the waiter *kills* me!' As Tracy rose the roomful of hungry diners looked her way. So did Deborah Dunton and Lee Turgo. I watched as Helen took Berniece's hand and squeezed it. Hard.

Chapter Five

Speech

Tracy mounted the podium carefully on her high heels, arranging some notes in front of her. 'If I may have your attention!' We looked up. Tracy, in her black sequined armor, so energetic, well informed, so politically correct. 'It is my great pleasure to welcome you to the Reading Room of the Howard Blooming Lesbian and Gay Memorial Archive of San Francisco!'

Cheers shook the rafters; the painted goddess above us seemed to soar, her filmy gown billowing in the waves of applause.

'Fuck San Francisco,' I thought I heard Larry Boznian mumble. Fresca and Carla exchanged worried glances.

'Tonight, I want to welcome you all to this momentous occasion. Our history – our lesbian and gay history has been ignored, our books burned, our stories rewritten, our tongues silenced. But no more!'

More applause. Tracy beamed as the sound of three thousand hands clapping swelled and subsided.

'We must band together to fight for our right to exist! This library – this lesbian and gay library – will preserve our past, a past we have fought to uncover, a past we must fight to protect!'

'*Get ready for revisionism,*' Rose whispered.

'When we started this project fifteen years ago, it was just a dream.'

'*Yeah, it was a nightmare for the public library staff,*' Rose hissed.

'Eight hundred grant applications later, we appealed to our community . . .' Tracy droned on, cataloging the late night meetings, the endless fundraisers, the huge sacrifices of time and money that went into erecting the monumental edifice that housed our history.

'And tonight,' Tracy said, 'I am proud to say that over nine hundred of you here have donated one thousand dollars!'

'*Nine hundred thousand!*' I whistled. '*Almost a million!*'

'Please, donors, raise your hands!' Tracy called into the throng. Hands shot up from all over the room.

'And now, I'd like to present Larry Boznian, creator of the mural which spans the ceiling of our archive, creating a homo heaven, in the style of Michelangelo, for our brothers and sisters to enjoy for eternity!'

Mumble, mumble. Larry Boznian was such a newcomer! But then, as the audience began to look up at the startling frescoed figures above our head, the occasional clap was repeated, until a thunderous roar filled the room.

Larry Boznian stood up too quickly and lost his footing. He grabbed on to his chair, but then his hands found Fresca's shoulder and he steadied himself. Her hand covered his in reassurance.

'Cheers!' He raised a glass to the crowd and stumbled again.

Concerned murmurs rose up from the crowd. Larry Boznian was a genius. Larry Boznian was a drunk.

What was it like, the moment when you give your masterpiece to the public? Maybe Larry was happier painting, more comfortable with a brush in his hand and lying on his back? Which made me think about Fresca. How happy would *she* be on *her* back? Larry sat down again.

'Yes, we celebrate our lesbian and gay heritage with pride, brothers and sisters, *pride!*' The crowd burst into more applause and Tracy gave them enough leash to cause whatever was waiting in the kitchen to congeal. The head waiter was eating his knuckles by the kitchen door.

'After dinner, during dessert,' Tracy continued, 'I understand that we will be accepting acquisitions for the library. We will be happy to house Frances Cohen's original research notes on *Lesbo-Parthenogenesis*, the memorabilia of Berniece Able, and the final papers – ' she paused here for emphasis, 'of Howard Blooming!'

I felt the big gummy ball of tape, trapped in the canvas bag at my feet. The announcement resulted in shocked silence, then murmurs of delighted surprise. 'And now, for our main speaker of the evening, popular mystery novelist, Helen Thomas!'

Helen rose from her chair to applause, her skirt swinging in a circle as she turned to make her way to the podium. But Tracy Port took this moment to nod to a frantic waiter. Helen was just mounting the pulpit as scores of servers emerged from the kitchen, long lines of black-suited men balancing tray upon tray of clanking dishes.

Clearing her throat, Helen had just adjusted the mike when Tracy arrived back at the table. She was followed by a phalanx of obedient waiters who hovered around, pushing large covered platters in between the diners to the rhythm of Tracy's nod.

Service was family style, but the atmosphere wasn't. Nobody wanted to start passing the large, covered dishes, nor did anyone want to serve others while Helen was speaking. I heard Helen clear her throat loudly. The tall woman with the big voice usually had no trouble attracting the attention of a crowd. But the famished diners had been waiting too long for dinner.

'Well, I'm starving!' Tracy took the lid off one of the casseroles. She nearly dropped it, and made a noisy clatter which attracted the attention of several tables. But soon everyone was busy with their food, lifting the lids to reveal mounds of potatoes ready for each plate – and no one was paying any attention to Helen.

'When I was growing up in the projects – ' she began.

'*Too bad,*' Fresca's mouth came close to my ear as we eyed the potatoes. '*You have some good food in California, you know.*' Lee Turgo was smoldering, watching her lover struggling to project over the noisy diners. But it was hard not to watch dinner being revealed in the middle of each and every table.

'*Fish, fish, fish*' the crowd was muttering, passing platters and scraping serving spoons, making Helen's speech almost inaudible. '*Shh!*'

'I remember my great Aunt . . .' Helen was saying. Lee Turgo shot us all a warning glance but the situation was way out of control.

'*I am a vegetarian!*' Fresca confided, her warm breath and continued attention almost making me forget my loyalty to Helen. '*So is Larry! Completely vegan!*'

Completely smashed, I thought, eyeing the drunken painter with distaste. What *was* their relationship anyway? Bisexual?

'*No one really expects anything from the food tonight.*' I found myself patting Fresca's leg, the soft strings of her ragged Levis tangling with my fingers. '*Shh, let's listen to Helen.*'

I turned back to the podium, straining to hear Helen's words. What was she saying?

'The bookmobile in our neighborhood . . . the projects . . . window on the world . . .'

Helen was losing speed quickly. Her voice was crawling back into her throat. The sea of diners was groaning over the cod, the *Gratins Dauphinois* were exhausted and replenished by busy waiters; barboys were filling requests for extra drinks from the discouraged diners. How could Helen compete?

She gave up. She mumbled, she chanted, she raced angrily through her speech. And who could blame her? When Helen left the podium she was fuming. And she went straight to Tracy Port.

The *Gratin Dauphinois* had just been served up on to Tracy's plate. 'Are the potatoes in a dairy sauce?' Tracy wondered aloud, ignoring Helen's arrival.

'You have quite a sense of timing!' Helen sputtered, looming behind the Executive Director. Lee Turgo nervously knit her hands under the table.

'Wonderful speech.' Tracy forked a flaky morsel into her mouth, avoiding Helen's eyes.

'How would *you* know? How would *anyone* know? Could anyone even *hear* me up there?' The table fell quiet. Helen fell into a chair next to Lee, who put her hand over Helen's, but Helen shook it off.

'I'm sorry Helen,' Tracy explained in an offhand way. 'The head waiter was having trouble with the chef – the fish – '

'Fish! You think this floor wax covered flounder is *edible*? Pass me some potatoes!' Helen almost jerked the platter of potatoes out of Tracy's hands. I wondered for a horrible moment if she would hurl it at Tracy. But Helen was trying hard to get it together, concentrating on spooning potatoes on to her plate. Her hand was shaking badly.

'Are you sure this isn't a dairy sauce?' Tracy held a forkful of potatoes in front of her, looking at it strangely.

'No, there's no dairy, dear,' Renquist consoled her.

'Did you hear what I said, Tracy?' demanded Helen.

'Please, Helen,' Lee Turgo cautioned.

'Don't you *please Helen* me!' Lee gritted her teeth and looked into her lap, a swathe of hair covering her eyes. Poor Helen. I could see by the look on her face that she was close to tears.

'Excuse me,' she muttered, then raced out of the dining room. I watched the black skirt billowing behind her as she ran out of the hall, towards the wheelchair accessible restrooms whose signs were in fourteen languages. I picked up my canvas bag, slung it over my shoulder and went after her.

I found her repairing her lipstick in a quiet corner of the women's room. Her hand was shaking.

'It was nice of you to follow me out, Emma. But don't worry, I'll survive.' I looked at her face. She was taking it hard, however brave she sounded. 'Tracy's just a drama queen. She loves to make this kind of stupid trouble between couples. Her fling with Lee wasn't important. I know that. When push comes to shove, Tracy Port just ain't marriage material, Emma.' Her hand steadied on the tube.

'Who is?'

'You and Frances are doing okay, aren't you?'

'Sure,' I tried to push Fresca out of my mind. I watched Helen run her glossy, bronze lipstick over her lips. The motion seemed to make her calmer. Everything under control. The metallic color just matched the piping of her collar. An alarm bell was ringing in my head. Something was terribly missing, but before I could say anything Helen said 'Emma, I just need to be alone for a moment.'

She screwed the lipstick back and lit a cigarette. I gave her a quick hug. Then I left her there, smoking and thinking. I hoped it did her some good.

I returned to the table to find Fresca propping up Larry Boznian in his chair.

'Maybe you'd better send him home in a cab.' I suggested.

'No, he'll be okay. Just a few minutes now. He will get better.' None the less Fresca was looking decidedly concerned. 'I'm so worried about him,' she confessed.

'The artistic community here in San Francisco has not been at all supportive of his work,' Carla Ribera flicked her long black curls back in disgust.

'It's just that Larry's an outsider; people are like that everywhere,' replied Fresca with resignation.

'Oh, San Francisco is so provincial! I mean,' Carla snorted, 'it's a pretty town and nice to *look* at, but what is there to *do* here?'

'You used to like it, Carla,' Rose said softly. Her voice held no rancor, only sadness. 'You used to live here.'

'Do you think the potatoes had any dairy?' Something in Tracy's voice made everyone look up. Her voice was loud, almost afraid. Forks stopped in mid-air. Conversation stopped. 'I think these potatoes have dairy – '

'Tracy, what is it?' Deborah leaned towards the Executive Director. Tracy looked ill.

'Tracy?' Renquist's voice went up a notch.

'Tracy!' Deborah breathed.

The Executive Director of the Archive looked very ill indeed. Her face had paled to an unnatural, waxy white. Slowly, silverware was lowered to the table. People looked at each other. At the plates of food.

'She's dreadfully allergic to dairy!' Deborah screeched, and I noticed, for the first time, a medical alert bracelet on Tracy's wrist. She was starting to fold at the waist, a spasm suddenly jerking her body into a grotesque fetal position.

'Does she have a hypo?' I jumped up and, holding the canvas bag with one hand, I opened Tracy's purse with the other. I began rifling through her personal effects. People with deadly allergies often carried a hypodermic syringe and adrenalin in case of an allergic reaction. Too bad Frances wasn't here. But inside Tracy's purse were just Kleenexes, a wallet, Dramamine, two tubes of lipstick and the tinfoil of an after dinner mint.

'Oh my God, Tracy!' Deborah shrieked and we all watched as the librarian's face began to tell a nightmare of a story. Tracy's teeth clenched together and then her mouth flew open. Her tongue was waggling, her eyes rolling back into her head. Her hands became claws and grabbed at her own throat.

A confused buzz filled the hall. People were pointing in our direction, craning their heads, rubbernecking, seeking the better view for neighbors who asked anxiously, 'What's happening?'

Tracy fell to the floor.

'Honey, don't, don't – ' Deborah was grabbing Tracy's wrists, trying to keep her ex-lover's nails from scratching the short neck from which a strange gurgling sound emanated. Tracy was trying to say something. Her eyes looked beyond Deborah, searching the table.

Lee Turgo was a frozen pillar of salt, terrified that Tracy was reaching out to her. Larry Boznian, suddenly sober, stared at Tracy's stricken face. Renquist had his arms outstretched and for a moment Tracy's hands responded, moving towards him, as if he could catch her. Her fingernails clawed the air. They were turning blue.

'Is there a doctor in the house? A nurse?' Rose was shouting at the top of her voice. The other diners were putting down their knives and forks. Slowly, they started to stand and move over towards us. One by one, a slow, horrible march of the curious towards the macabre.

'A doctor, a doctor – a paramedic? A fucking NURSE!' Rose cried, waving her arms up and down, a morse code of mortality. 'A doctor, a nurse – '

'I'm a doctor,' said a small woman moving forwards through the crowd. Her tiny hands found Tracy's neck and searched for pulse points, as some terrible force seemed to take Tracy completely. She was a puppet with invisible strings being jerked without pity. The doctor stepped out of her way.

'I'll hold her down!' Deborah cried.

'No, she's convulsing, you might dislocate her shoulder,' the doctor ordered, leaning over Tracy's tortured body again. We all watched as Tracy's face turned ashen and her lips became a dark, teal blue, just like Carla Ribera's suit. Her jerking subsided, her eyes rolled back into her head and the sounds ceased.

'She has environmental illness – it must be something in the building!' Deborah looked up at the fresco, as if the paint were responsible. 'Do something!' Deborah screeched at the doctor, at all of us.

The doctor stopped her probing and looked into Tracy's face, pulling up her eyelid and then closing it again. 'She's dead.'

'Dead?' Deborah repeated.

'Dead?' the crowd gasped. Tracy was dead?

'No dairy. I didn't think there was – ' Renquist sounded defensive through his shocked tones. 'No dairy, no dairy . . .'

'This was no allergic reaction,' the little doctor said. Then she picked up Tracy's plate of potatoes and sniffed them carefully. 'Smells like almonds,' she said.

'She's not allergic to *almonds*,' breathed Deborah.

It would take a moment for the concept to take hold, but I knew what the doctor meant. Renquist didn't have to worry about his menu advice, and Tracy wasn't allergic to almonds, or to anything in the building. Environmentally sensitive or not, everyone is allergic to cyanide.

We all stood there, a silent guard over the woman who had created the Howard Blooming Lesbian and Gay Memorial Archive, the event becoming more historic than any of us would have liked.

Just then Helen returned from the bathroom, her lips freshly bronzed, her composure regained. She made an opening in the wall of tuxedos which stood over Tracy's body, the large skirt of her dress throwing a shadow over Tracy's black sequins. 'What?' she breathed softly.

'Almonds,' the doctor said. 'Cyanide.'

I remembered my interview with Helen in the bathroom and I watched as her hands traveled up to her neck and made the unhappy discovery. 'No!' she cried, 'What? Oh no!' She was almost laughing. But there wasn't anything funny to laugh about.

Helen Thomas' Romanov period amulet was gone. She was quick to conceal the look on her face. Quietly Helen Thomas let go of Lee Turgo's hand and faded back into the crowd.

Chapter Six

Potatoes

Cyanide poisoning has been called 'internal asphyxia'. The victim is strangled from within, as the body's red blood cells are prevented from absorbing oxygen. Tracy Port, whose every cell had been instantly starved of air, now lay inert at the feet of the dressed-up diners; the shocked participants in what was supposed to be one of the brightest moments in our community's development.

'Call an ambulance!' The doctor said, although her heart was not in it. She was probably required to call an ambulance; the paramedics would call the coroner. Tracy's heart was stilled and Deborah Dunton let out a wail which would put all previous primal therapy to shame.

'Tracy, Tracy,' Renquist Falkenberg knelt down beside her still body, a dark shape that no longer shuddered. A person we knew, that we couldn't believe was dead. Renquist reached out tentatively to touch Tracy and then pulled his hand quickly away. David Sing, the crime scene inspector, was approaching at a brisk, professional trot.

What luck, a queer cop on the scene of the biggest murder in the lesbian and gay community since Howard Blooming had been shot.

I knew Renquist and David would quickly take control of the situation. David Sing was already busy securing the area: pushing back the tuxedos, leaving Tracy on the floor, like the Wicked Witch of the West; a house just landed on her and nothing the doctor could do.

'What happened?' David asked the physician.

'Poisoning,' the woman said. 'Cyanide.'

'All right, clear the area, step back.'

'Let the officer do his work,' Renquist intoned to those of us too shocked to fully comprehend what was happening. 'The proper authorities are here on the scene and will take care of everything. They will tell us what to do.'

'It's over now,' David called out, pushing back the crowd. His back was turned away from the table. I looked around for Helen. She was in a corner with Lee Turgo. The pendant was gone. Helen's fingers couldn't find it, even as they desperately searched. I could see her fingers underneath a film of black silk exploring the space between her breasts, in case, just in case, the chain had broken and it had fallen and gotten trapped between bosom and brassiere. She was sputtering. I had a very bad taste in my mouth. Helen, I was sure, had been framed.

I dropped to the floor, looking for anything, any clue that might get Helen off the hook. With one hand I clutched the bag with Howard's memorabilia, with the other I turned over dropped napkins and combed through crumbs.

There wasn't a pendant, but there was something else. A brown rectangle. A leather lump. A thick wallet. I picked it up, the worn leather still warm, describing the shape of some ass which had sat on it for years and years. I flipped it open and my fingers snaked through the contents. A folded receipt from Streetlight Records – Classical CDs. Four credit cards, three condoms, two hundred dollars in cash. It could have been the wallet of any of thousands of gay men in San Francisco. Except that the embossed name on the credit cards read 'Renquist Falkenberg'. Renquist's wallet, complete with just-in-case condoms, had nearly been donated to a crime scene investigator. I heard the distant whine of an ambulance and put the wallet in my pocket.

David Sing was waiting for me as I emerged from under the table. 'What are you doing Emma?'

'Lost my earring.'

'Just keep the fuck outta here, do you mind?' The young officer was getting angry and I had no interest in pushing him over the edge. I stepped back into the clot of people and faded backwards out of the room. I took the opportunity to change clothes in the bathroom.

In the cold light of the white-tiled chamber, the sequined dress was ejected in favor of baggy cotton pants. I pulled the turtleneck on, opening up the zipper around the neck. Things were too hot at the Gala Dinner. And I had a hot moment or two ahead to get some vital things done. I left the cubicle and returned to find Deborah Dunton, holding the dead Tracy Port in her arms.

Tracy's face was achieving a bright pink color, as red blood cells rushed to the surface of her skin. Even dead, her body mounted a last-ditch attempt to find air.

'Salmon bisque,' slurred a voice next to me. Larry Boznian.

'What?'

'Jussa color.'

'I've heard lighter patter from the coroner.'

But one could expect a lot of strange behavior at the scene of a murder. The most devastated person could crack the worst jokes, and a murderer could do a wailing aria that would please the best crime scene conductor. Innocent women were frequently fingered for not being emotional enough.

Dunton was covering her tracks there. She was the only one, in fact, who seemed truly upset that Tracy was no longer with us.

'Get back! Get Back!' David Sing was calling out with authority, his hands in front of him as the crowd receded from the pink-hued horror in the black sequined dress. Someone screamed. Someone sobbed. A flashbulb popped.

I was still holding the black canvas bag when I heard Berniece cry out. 'The scrapbook! The scrapbook!'

Searching frantically around their chairs, Allen and Berniece looked for the large, embroidered book which

Berniece had intended to donate to the Archive. 'The scrapbook – you were holding it, right?' Allen asked Berniece.

Berniece's voice acquired a certainty and a volume that made us all turn around. 'Carla *you stole my scrapbook!*' Berniece was leaning over her walker, pointing at the fashion photographer in her Edwardian-cut coat.

'Don't be ridiculous!' Carla was returning from the washroom. The fresh lipstick on her mouth glistened as she smiled quizzically at the old poet. 'What *are* you talking about, Berniece?' Carla's hands were stuffed deeply in the pockets of her long-tailed coat.

'I said, Carla, that my scrapbook is gone. When Tracy – and we were all watching – ' Berniece spluttered but the blank look on Carla's face confused her for a moment. 'I distinctly remember you coming over to my chair and – and – '

'Berniece, I'm sorry. I don't know what you're talking about. Did you lose something?'

'Carla,' she said firmly, 'I'm certain you took it!'

Carla sighed and rolled her eyes. Lee Turgo tightened her mouth. 'C'mon, Berniece. Let's go home. Where's Helen?'

Then the City Supervisor appeared, back from the restroom. 'Here's your wallet, Renquist.'

'Oh-my-God, *here* it is!' He didn't check for credit cards or theft, just put it quickly in the inside breast pocket of his jacket.

'Now if the rest of you will please give your name and address to the officer at the door.' David Sing was trying to clear the room. 'Emma, that means you, *move it!*'

The whining of a far-distant ambulance began. As it grew louder my task became clearer. Whatever had or hadn't happened to Berniece's scrapbook, I realized what I must do. Soon the place would be crawling with cops. Everyone and everything would be under scrutiny. If Howard had wanted his journals sealed for sixty years, I certainly didn't want the cops taking custody of them. I remembered the old safe that was in the basement. The nineteenth-century safe that had been donated by a gay banker, full of metal boxes; each of which could only be opened or locked by two finely wrought keys used in unison. Howard would have loved it.

I rushed through the dining room, past the tables with plates of battered, gray cod lying limp on the trays, eyes gazing at Larry Boznian's ceiling. Tracy dead! I held the canvas bag tightly. The concrete corridors stretched endlessly under my feet.

I ran down the internal stairs into the basement, three steps at a time. I found the double doors which would lead me into the reception area of the vault. The lock of the double door was easy to foil. Too many hinges and too much play where the doors met made quick work for the slim jim. I was still breathless when I entered the vault.

There were all of Helen's manuscripts. Her fight with Tracy flashed into my mind. So did Allen staring at the box containing Howard's final papers. I walked over to the safe, its foot-thick door open, inviting. The keys were waiting in deposit box locks. I had only to chose.

I gazed over the metal containers and chose one large enough for the tape-covered package. I opened my canvas bag and pulled it out. I looked at it mournfully. How could I put Howard's journals away for sixty whole years? But it had to be done.

I turned one of the keys and pulled. A large metal drawer slid towards me. I took one last look at the tape-covered box; I got a ballpoint pen and wrote my initials on the surface, over the joins of tape. Now there would be no way someone could unwrap the tape and rewrap it without my knowing.

I placed the box in the drawer and watched it disappear as I slid the drawer closed. I turned the key to lock once and turned the second key in the other direction to complete the procedure. Then I put the keys into my bra, where the metal was cold against my nipples, and zipped up the neck of my sweater. Mission accomplished.

Then I remembered Frances' notes on *Lesbo-Parthenogenesis*. What had happened to them? A feeling of dread crept over me.

I hadn't seen the collection of notebooks since I'd first sat down to dinner. Frances' careful observations on grid paper were gone. My hands felt around inside the canvas bag. But I had been carrying *Lesbo-Parthenogenesis* separately. Oh, no.

Dunton would say it was hidden aggression. Frances had gone off without me and left me with her notes. So I lost them. As hundreds of others have lost significant artifacts belonging to their lovers. Manuscripts. Paintings. All through time lovers have lost things entrusted to their care by the beloved. Hidden aggression? Hidden or obvious, the notes were gone.

Then I smelled cloves and leather. Fresca Alcazon was right behind me, short of breath.

'What are you doing?' she asked.

'Getting a breath of fresh air.'

'In a vault?' she said sardonically, raising an eyebrow.

'Well, you know, I've never seen anyone die like that.' I watched her closely. 'Right in front of my eyes.'

Fresca's eyebrow fell and I regretted my snippy tone. Her lip was quivering. 'I can't believe Tracy's dead.' Her lips sealed together, keeping some emotion tight to herself. She bent her head and before I knew it my fingers had found their way into her mass of dark brown hair. She leaned towards me, or did I pull her to me? Somehow we were holding each other.

'Did you know Tracy?' My voice was soft. I breathed a sweet scent in from her hair. Gently, she pushed me away. I peered into her face. She was composing herself quickly.

'Sort of,' she explained. 'I have an original copy of Gertrude Stein's *The Making of Americans*. One of a limited edition of five copies. Japanese vellum, lettered in gold.' I watched her caraway seed eyes glisten for a moment. This woman loved books. 'An author's copy. I guess it must be

63

worth a lot. Larry invited me to the Gala and I thought I would donate it to the Archive.'

'A very nice gesture.'

Fresca shrugged her shoulders. 'It seemed like the right thing to do. I travel a lot. What do I need with a first edition?'

'It's still a nice thing to do.'

'Anyway, I got in touch with Tracy. She invited me to sit at the VIP table.'

'You really like Gertrude Stein?'

'She's *wonderful*. Some people find her tough going, but that's because they don't listen to her words. They don't take the time to linger. You almost have to go into a trance, read passages out loud, to understand.'

'Okay.' I still had the smell of Fresca's hair on my hands. 'Recite something. Something pertinent to the situation here.'

Fresca looked at me. 'No, really, I – '

'Come on.' Howard Blooming's notes were safely locked away, the keys cold against my heart. Frances was in Seattle. I smiled at Fresca. 'Don't be shy. I want to hear Stein's words.'

'Okay.' Fresca looked over at the old safe. She seemed to be gathering inspiration, not counting keys. Her mouth went slack, her eyelids closed.

When the words came I saw why she had been irritated with Larry Boznian. Larry Boznian's clipped accent and whiny voice had nothing on the deep, sonorous tones of Fresca Alcazon. She touched the mole at the base of her neck for a second, put her hand in the pocket of what was left of her jeans and began to recite.

'*History there – is no disaster – Those who make history – Cannot be overtaken – As they will make – History which they do – because it is necessary – That every one will – Begin to know that – They must know that – History is what it is – Which it is as they do – *'

She stopped mid-sentence and looked at me. I knew

we were going to kiss. All the tumblers and teasers of combinations in all the safes in the world couldn't compete with Fresca. She reached out for me, her arms long, her hands confident. I felt those hands behind my back, her fingertips knitting naturally behind my waist. She pulled me towards her and I could feel the warmth of her body through her tattered garments. I wouldn't be able to get away easily. Her breath was hot on my neck.

'Not and now, now and not, not and now, by and by not and now, as not, as soon as not, not and now, now as soon now, now as soon, now as soon as soon as now.' Fresca's legs were hard, her body strong, thin and sharp as a knife. I twisted away.

'C'mon,' I took her hands and pulled her away from the safe. I put my hands on the metal door and pushed. It slipped neatly and quietly on its oiled hinges into its stainless steel frame. I pulled up the big handle, hearing a satisfying thud deep within the door. I spun the combination lock around. A roulette wheel that no one could beat. I hoped. We left the vault, the double doors relocking behind us.

The reading room upstairs was now an official crime scene, roped off by yellow caution tape and crawling with cops taking notes and photographs. In the distance the popping of flashbulbs illuminated the pink bubble that had been Tracy's face. David Sing strolled back and forth talking to his colleagues. I scanned the room and saw Helen Thomas, huddled confusedly in the corner of the room. Berniece Able and Lee Turgo were giving their names to an officer.

'Hey, look.' A big voice boomed over those gathered by the table. I drew closer, Fresca sticking closely by my side. 'What's this?' It was Renquist's voice cutting through the din. He was looking aghast at the dining room table where Tracy's potatoes were being picked over, by a cop putting samples from the table into little glass tubes. But that was not what Renquist was referring to.

An officer had lifted a napkin on the table and everyone pressed around to see what lay underneath. It was a split shard of amber and a piece of filigree work as lovely as a Tiffany egg. Inside, a crystal was split like a piece of rock candy. Grandmother's poison.

David Sing picked up the piece of crystal with a pair of tweezers. He peered at it closely, then sniffed. He inspected the plate of potatoes, bringing his face close to the dish and then returned his gaze to the pendant.

'Whose necklace is this?' he asked loudly. No one needed to answer. We all looked at Helen. She seemed suddenly very alone; a tall frightened figure in funereal black.

'Come here please.' David beckoned at her. From across the room Helen came towards us with long strides. But she was shaken.

'This is your necklace?' David asked her.

'Yes.' Helen breathed the word as if this were a bad dream. 'I just noticed it was missing.'

'Are you aware that this necklace seems somehow to have been contaminated with a poisonous substance?'

'Well, there's a sort of myth about this piece of jewelry.'

'I'm going to have to ask you to come downtown for questioning,' David informed her. He was all business now. I moved in closer.

'Helen, don't say anything!' I advised. David turned to me with a furious look. A cop took Helen's arm and held on to her tight.

'*You have the right to remain silent . . .* '

Lee Turgo was at my side. 'Emma.' She grabbed my shoulder. Her grip was vice-like. Her hand kept pushing back the shock of auburn hair. 'Emma, I have to talk to you.'

'*. . . anything you say from this point on can and will be used against you . . .* '

'You work for Willie Rossini. Tell her, you just tell her, I'll hire her to prove Helen innocent. Anything, anything . . .'

I put my hand on Lee's arm. 'Don't worry. I'll get a call in to Willie immediately. I'm sure she'll represent Helen.' I looked over again at Helen, surrounded now by a circle of cops. Her entire face and body were stiff. 'Don't worry, Lee. We'll get her out on bail, within twenty-four hours. She can talk to Willie in the morning.'

'. . . *will be used against you in a court of law* . . . '

The sheriffs were deciding which one of them would handcuff her. Helen's eyes widened as two women came closer, the shining cuffs snapping around the delicate silk tulle gathered at Helen's wrists.

It was too neat. Too tidy. And the whole romantic mess of the Olivia Cruise had been too public, too easily exploited. I remembered my conversation with Helen in the bathroom after her fiasco of a speech. The amulet had gone by then. It could have been eased off her neck at any time, by anyone, during one of those many hugs and kisses that the evening had afforded.

I watched Carla Ribera helping to escort a drunken Larry Boznian into the night. Fresca Alcazon had disappeared. Rose was wheeling her chair into an elevator at the far end of the Reading Room. The doors slid quietly closed behind her.

Lee Turgo, her hands stuffed in her pockets, was staring at the toes of her wing-tips. Berniece Able stood next to her, an icon, now thoroughly distraught and confused.

I would find out who had killed Tracy Port, I thought. And I had a good hunch that it wouldn't be Helen Thomas.

Chapter Seven

Diet Fresca

I met Rose out on the pavement.

'Who will be Executive Director now?' she asked me.

'Who do you think?'

'Deborah Dunton? She's the President of the Board. The natural successor. I wonder if she murdered Tracy?'

'Rose, the murderer could have been any one of us at that table. Or a dozen people who weren't even there.'

The nasty tones of a drunken argument wafted over to us on the evening air. In the distance I saw Fresca Alcazon, Carla and Larry Boznian huddling together. The silhouettes of Larry Boznian's ears stood out like two big fins. He was having a hard time getting the words out and what he did get out wasn't worth listening to. Carla Ribera was alternately admonishing and pleading with him. At one point he grabbed Fresca's arm violently. She shook it off even more violently. She looked strong in the streetlight, looked strong fighting off Larry Boznian.

The drunken, clipped British tones of Larry Boznian reached us. 'I don't want you to go off and lie in any *guttahs.*'

I hoped he wasn't talking about me.

But he was. Fresca was on her way over. The rags on her arms blew in the evening breeze, revealing long, developed biceps. Something heavy bumped against her hip.

'*Fresca, fuck yew, yew little creep!*' It was Larry Boznian's voice. He was very, very, drunk. Carla threw up her arms and walked away, her long black curls tossing on her back as she strode swiftly up the hill to her car. Larry Boznian stood alone, screaming after the two women in the darkness.

As Fresca stepped into the circle of light I could tell she had been crying. She looked very sad. And very young. I didn't feel great myself.

'Can I take you home, Emma?' Fresca Alcazon was breaking through my defenses like a burglar.

It was a cold and lonely night. It wasn't a night to spend alone. Fresca caught something in my eye that I couldn't hide fast enough. As she saw her chances improve she smiled. It wasn't a made-for-consumption politician smile. It wasn't an approval-seeking or slippery, butter smile either. It was a young, and even innocent smile. It hit me like a curve ball I couldn't avoid.

'This is your place?' Fresca looked up at the flat-faced Victorian duplex.

'Yeah, thanks for the ride.'

And what a ride it had been. Fresca's transport was a 500cc BMW bike. I had clung to her back on the way home, the fringe from her leather jacket brushing my lips – a leathery French kiss.

'Could I – do you think I could use your phone?'

'Sure.' I said it lightly, but I knew I should have said no. If I let Fresca Alcazon into my house on a night like this, it would be a miracle if I saw the dawn alone.

But I took Fresca inside and pointed out the phone, then wandered outside and sat on the stairs. Helen was probably just getting booked. Someone would be grabbing her beautiful fingers, roughly pressing her fingertips on to a police blotter. It was a Friday night and Friday night could be busy down at the jail. I wondered what kind of cell mates Helen would get. It would be early. Maybe she'd get lucky.

I remembered the scene in the library vault. All those manuscript pages. And the condescension of Tracy Port. How could anyone ever have been in love with her?

I wondered what the lab analysis of Helen's pendant

would reveal. I should get one of Rose's researchers to look into everything that had been written about that amulet. Perhaps an appraiser had indicated something about the contents that could help Helen? Perhaps I should read *Grandmother's Poison* again.

I looked up at the sky, the same sky which stretched above us all. Me, Fresca, Frances. Frances, up in Seattle. Frances whose notes I'd lost. Frances, somewhere in Seattle, with all those eager, fertile lesbians. They'd be hopeful – some single – some no doubt dying to bed the doctor who might give women the power of independent creation – if not the orgasm of their rainy, lonely Seattle lives. We had started talking about 'opening up our relationship.' 'Opening.' Like opening a can of worms, only these worms would have serpent heads, spiked fangs that could cut to the quick and eyes that only flashed yellow. Frances the Amazon doctor, potential miracle worker, would have a lot of amorous opportunity on the road.

I shook myself. Frances and I were fine, just fine. It was good to have Fresca here. But only because she was a suspect for the murder of Tracy Port, just like everyone else who'd been at the VIP table at the Gala Dinner. There was a lot about Fresca that didn't add up. I would ask her some questions, and that was all.

I sat up straight and tried to clear my head of lustful thoughts. I went inside to the roll-top secretary and pulled out a cardboard envelope, the kind used to mail computer disks. I took out a label and addressed it to myself. Then I slipped my hand into my bra and drew out one of the now-warm keys, leaving the other one pressed against my skin. I sealed the envelope, slid it under a number of other envelopes that were ready to be mailed, and returned to the kitchen.

I found Fresca with my receiver pressed hard to her ear. How long was she going to be on the phone? Her eyes were quiet under the cloud of dark brown hair. Her hands fingered the threads on her jeans into complicated patterns. Did she *know* she was beautiful?

I wondered what her ethnic heritage was. With her Asian eyes and African nose, Fresca's face was a history of continents and people. She was the Age of Aquarius child. Her face registered something painful. 'I'm really sorry about that,' she said. 'But I can't help it. You'll have to work it out by yourself this time, *cara*.'

I shook myself again. It wasn't a good idea to stand and watch her counting the holes in her clothes: I needed distracting. Besides, there was healthcare work to do. Outside, four large marijuana plants had just reached their blooming potential, and Marijuana Madeline was coming tomorrow to pick them up.

I went down the back stairs with a machete and cut the plants down, then dragged the thick stems with their star-shaped leaves and aromatic flowers back up to the apartment. Fresca was still listening to whoever it was on the other end of the phone. She mumbled something. In Italian.

Engrossing myself happily in the dusky, cloying-scented blooms, I clipped off the larger fan leaves and threw them away in the kitchen garbage. Finding the brown paper grocery bags which would allow the buds to cure without molding, I slipped the long aromatic skewers inside. Marijuana Madeline would be coming tomorrow, would continue to cure the pot in a different location before distributing it to cancer and AIDS patients.

Fresca had wandered as far as the static would allow her on the cordless phone. Before I could blink she was in Frances' office. I crept behind her into the doorway.

Tap, tap, tap. Those long, broad-tipped fingers tapped on the hardened plastic of the phone as her eyes flickered over Frances' bulletin board. There, more notes on the latest developments in ovum division were displayed in scientific hieroglyphics. Surely Fresca could not understand them – but she was nodding, perhaps in agreement with the voice on the phone. I saw her hand reach out, towards Frances'

Rolodex. Before her fingers could walk further I interrupted her.

'Can I help you?'

The jeans jumped high enough to clear a low hurdle. Fresca's face hid surprise. And something else, something I caught before she composed her face. That something was fear. She pressed the button which hung up the phone and asked 'Is this your office?'

'No, it's not my office, and you know it.'

'Huh?'

'I'm hardly the scientific type.'

'What type are you?'

'The type that doesn't like strangers wandering through my house.'

'Am I a stranger?'

'Yes.'

She looked at me in silence.

'What exactly is your business in San Francisco, Fresca?'

'I've told you what my business is. I've come to give the Stein book to the Archive.'

'So what's your connection with Larry Boznian?'

'Christ, Emma! What is this? The third degree? I came here because I thought you liked me. Now you say I'm a stranger and bark questions at me!'

'Just checking out the scene –'

Just to cap the evening of poisoned potatoes and marital mayhem, Fresca started crying hard. Tears crawled down her buttery cheeks. She took hold of my hand and brought it up to her face, like it was something precious. Like I was someone she knew. Someone who would look after her and make everything all right.

'Listen, Emma. I need a place to stay. Just for tonight. Please – could I sleep on your couch?'

There was a sinking feeling in my stomach. We both knew what would happen next.

'I just need a place to sleep. I really need a place to sleep.'

We stood in silence, my hand still held against her cheek. My hand moved into a nest of fuzz at the nape of her neck. My lucky lips found the delicate jawbone, the softly moving mouth.

'Oh Emma.' We were really kissing now. Fresca's kisses were slow motion. Her tongue investigated my mouth, then my shoulder, my hands. Then she stopped.

'Hey, what's that – that *smell*?' she pulled back, staring at my fingers. I knew which aroma was clinging to my nails; the potent pollen of my backyard crop was infusing my hands with a heady post-harvest scent.

'It's pot,' I explained.

'What?'

'I grow it.'

'You're a *grower*?'

'Just a few plants out in the garden. I just brought them up. They were females that looked ready to develop seeds.' I stopped at the look of concern on Fresca's face. 'Don't worry,' I explained, 'it's for cancer and AIDS patients. I've got three full bags on the counter in the kitchen. Five months of careful cultivation. Hey, you're not going to go all twelve-step on me, are you?'

'*A year of grass is a year of alas. When grass grows that is all that grows but grass is grass and alas and alas is alas.*'

'When in doubt, quote Gertrude Stein.'

'Dope is for dopes, Emma.'

'I'll put you in the guest room,' I said.

The guest room was filled with all the Day of the Dead artifacts from the Mexican vacations Frances and I took annually. I left Fresca standing there, looking at the bed while I went to bring her a clean towel. When I came back she was sitting on the edge of the bed. Murmuring. '*When she shuts her eyes – she sees the green things – among which she has been working – and then as she falls asleep – she sees them a little different. The green things then have black roots – and the black roots – have red stems and then she is exhausted –*'

73

She stopped reciting when she saw me. Her eyes were soft, and calm now. She took a deep breath, then let it out with a smile that was almost a laugh. She didn't take her eyes off mine. There was a question there. I moved towards her. My lips gave her the answer.

The apartment of my marriage floated away from us. There was only Fresca and myself, and the Mexican skeletons, carved from coconut husks, cast out of sugar, winking with glitter-filled eyes at the way our hands found each other. Delightful surprises in hard thighs, long, sculpted feet, lengthy arms and a sometimes gentle, sometimes demanding touch.

Fresca's hands were nearing the dangerous centers of my breasts, where I had left one key to the locked box in the safe in the Archive. 'Your arms are so beautiful,' Fresca mumbled. In the candlelight, her birthmark glowed like a ruby, pulsing with the quickening beat of her heart.

Fresca's soft, panther skin rippled over ribs. That strong back which I'd clung on to while riding her bike moved under me. Fresca's breasts were large, they would swing, I thought, when released from the athletic bra underneath her shirt. I eased her away to take off her leather jacket. My hands found their way through the sieve of denim. Oh, oh. Adultery was just as I remembered it. It was wonderful.

A laughing skeleton whizzed by on a bicycle. Fresca's mouth was watering, her hands had moved safely away from my breasts. I kissed those obedient fingers, and heard the chuckling of a mask, saw the wink of eye sockets which were only holes. Dead ancestors, like Tracy Port, like Howard Blooming. I was losing my concentration. I drank in another Fresca kiss. But I couldn't help thinking about all that had gone on before, this evening. The Gala Dinner for the Lesbian and Gay Memorial Archive. The night that Tracy Port was poisoned, Helen was arrested, and the first night that I stepped out of my marriage. Concentrate.

'*You like this best,*' she murmured. '*Lock me in nearly. Unlock me sweetly, I love my baby with a rush rushingly.*'

My fingers found their way down the buttons of what was left of her Levis. She slid them off. They seemed to fall away from legs as long and brown as I had hoped, with lovely down about four inches above the ankle. The legs, however, were not a matched pair.

I drew in my breath. Etiquette demanded that I not ask questions, but I could see that something horrible had happened to Fresca. Something had eaten away the lower half of her calf. A quilted series of patches covered it; brown skin, pink skin. Fresca pulled her leg up underneath her. A mottled mess that was none of my business. Something about that leg set off a bell. But I had no idea why.

My next kiss was guilty and then I pushed her, as gently as I could, away from me. 'Not now, okay?'

'Aww,' she crooned. She closed her eyes and reached out for me like a child. A strong child. Her hands were velvet, my skin was silk, her skin was satin, my hands were black leather. I pushed her away more firmly.

'Okay, okay.' Fresca took a deep breath. I watched the course of her breathing slow down. She curled into my arms and I found myself holding her hand, squeezing the tips of her long, broad fingers.

'I really like you, Emma. I really like you a lot, a lot, a lot,' Fresca murmured in resigned disappointment. Then her breathing became so heavy I knew she was beyond words.

I stared into the cloudy chaos of her dark, honey-colored hair, as I felt her fall into dreams. She still smelled of cloves and clean, sun-dried cotton. And now she was sleeping, leaving me to the privacy of my own thoughts. I had a lot of them.

My foot reached down for the nest of disintegrated blue jeans and pulled it slowly towards me. I reached into the back pocket. I opened up a wallet and saw the driver's license of Eleanor DeWade, who, if I was to believe the picture pasted there, was also sleeping next to me.

That's when the thought hit me. *Me.*

Could it be that the poisoner had been confused? Perhaps

a professional killer, posing as a waiter, had instructions to kill the woman in the black sequined dress. The woman who was holding Howard Blooming's notes. Maybe Tracy's death was a mistake.

I pushed myself up off the bed. Fresca was sleeping on her stomach, sprawled out now, as if she didn't have a care in the world. As if she was used to having a bed to herself all the time. She snored. Okay.

Her leather jacket was on the floor in the corner. I remembered how I had eased it off her shoulders, how she had helped me take it off and flung it far out of reach. I dove down under the eave and retrieved it. Inside I found what I had suspected was there. Something I had thought I noticed while clinging to Fresca on the bike ride home.

A little gun.

A .22, nothing to get too worked up about. Better than a BB, but you couldn't kill anybody with it. Not right off. If you were a good aim you could take them out at the knees though. A nice little gun, if you knew exactly how to use it.

I rotated the cylinder. It was empty. I put the unloaded gun far under the bed. Then I sat on the carpet and looked out the window, away from the flickering candles. Had Renquist hugged Fresca? No, Fresca had pushed him away, I remembered.

'YAWWW!' Fresca Alcazon's screech split the sequence of dinner replay. Wide awake, bolt upright, with her eyes wide open but seeing nothing, this woman, this stranger, was screaming in the darkness, in my bed, in my arms.

'Where am I?' she demanded, looking around her as if she didn't recognize the bedroom, the Day of the Dead artifacts, or me.

'Larry!' she cried, looking straight in front of her, staring into the flame of the nearest candle and seeing, not the room, but a chaos which terrified her. I blew out the candles and turned on the overhead light. Every corner was flooded with unrelenting brightness as I said, 'Hey, take it easy.' I held Fresca by her shoulders and pushed a fuzzy mat of hair out of her face, finding her eyes and holding them there.

'Oh, so it's *you*, okay,' she breathed quietly.

'You don't have to worry about *me*. *I'm* not armed.'

But before Fresca had time to think about what I was saying our conversation was interrupted.

'Thump! Thump!'

Fresca, poised above me, froze, her lips parted, as if she knew the moment was coming. 'Quiet!' she hissed at me, as if this was her house.

'Thunk! Thunk!'

There was no doubt about it. Somebody was walking on the roof of the building. Fresca leapt off the bed and tore into the kitchen. I heard paper bags being torn open, and the toilet flushing; gurgling over and over.

'Wait!' I cried, but it was too late. I heard the jiggle of the handle, metal and porcelain, again and again and I knew what had happened. Fresca had contributed all my homegrown Hemp for Health to the sewage system of San Francisco.

'Cool it, will you? It could be anything on that roof! It could be my cat!'

'Yeah, a 180 pound cat. I'm not staying here and getting busted!'

I went over to the bathroom sill and leaned outside. The garden behind the house was quiet, free of lurking shadows. I went back to the bedroom, peered up, over the gable, to the upstairs apartment. Laura was home. I went downstairs and walked outside around the entire house. I took a flashlight and examined the hard dry lawn for something, I didn't know what.

Then I walked back up to my apartment through the decimated garden. Fresca was ready to leave.

'You have an exciting life, Emma. I think I can do without it.'

'Yours doesn't seem so straightforward either.' I wondered how she would do without her .22. We locked eyes for a moment, lust, anger and frustration a high-octane fuel that was getting us nowhere fast. Fresca threw on her leather jacket and, without checking the pockets, was gone.

Chapter Eight

Wrong Number

Dawn. The big orange ball was cracking, splitting open like a rotten egg on the sharp edge of Mount Diablo. I followed the glowing sphere as it split the darkness, its pink message whispering something obscene. I hadn't slept at all.

I'd spent the rest of the night trying to rescue my plants after Fresca's disposal operation. I managed one bud from the top of one plant. Then I'd started a new crop.

Marijuana seeds are not easy to sprout. I'd originally tried keeping them in damp soil and they thumbed their shells at me and never opened. Then I remembered the simple paper towel and jar method of seed sprouting from elementary school.

Soften them for days in the paper towel, fool them with a moist yogurt container in a cupboard right over the refrigerator where it's warm. The folded cloth on the sides of the container draw moisture up like a wick. Hot and wet, just like Fresca Alcazon.

Sometimes the summer-like Octobers would fool the otherwise annual plants and I could squeeze in two crops a year. And working with the plants gave me a contact high that was conducive to, if not deductive abilities, flashbacks, and a whole lot of feelings based on intuition.

I forced my thoughts back to the previous evening. To the moments before I'd met Helen in the bathroom when her amulet had been clearly missing from her neck. Had she been wearing it during her speech? That would be easy enough to find out. At the table, Helen was placed uncomfortably between Lee Turgo and Tracy Port. Renquist Falkenberg hugged everyone and lost his wallet. Larry Boznian acted as if he was very drunk. Fresca carried a .22 and someone had mugged me earlier that evening.

I walked into the bathroom and took off all my clothes. Sneak and creep clothes I'd slept in, if you could call it sleeping. The turtleneck was stale, and the pants needed a brushing. The bra was empty.

The second key was gone.

I ran to the basket where the mail was waiting. The self-addressed computer disk mailer waited patiently under the utility bill. I squeezed the cardboard together between my fingers. The other key was still inside.

I ran back to the guestroom and searched the floor inch by inch. I came up with Fresca's .22 and a lot of cat hair. I went down the stairs to the garden, through the weeds and back upstairs, examining each tread. Each stepping stone. No key.

The phone rang. Willie Rossini was on the line. 'Listen, I'm sorry to ring so early. But I've managed to get bail for Helen. She's entered a plea of not guilty. Pick her up, will you, Emma?'

I put the outgoing mail into a plastic sack and dropped it off at the Bryant Street Post Office on my way to the Hall of Justice. The letters would reach their destination on Monday. At the Hall of Justice I found a disheveled Helen, her black shirtwaist crushed and wilted, signing a receipt for the manila envelope which contained her personal belongings. She barely nodded to me as she signed the receipt.

'Lee's waiting for you at home.'

'Okay.'

Helen looked like many people look after their first night in jail. Reduced to a number, reduced to a series of functions, food tubes which must be locked up. A black star who had burnt out, Helen's face looked gray and grim.

'How'd you do in there?'

'Fine. I got more dialogue in a night than I could ever want.' Helen managed a smile. 'Two women were sobbing, three women were screaming and televisions were on until they turned the lights off.' Helen had deep blue lines under her eyes. 'They made us polish the handles of our cells this morning.' An ironic twist took over her lips.

'Don't worry, Helen. Willie feels confident she can get you off.'

'Then why do I feel like I'm going to be crushed by the wheels of white justice, Emma? I already have the tire tracks across my back.'

'Willie will make sure you never go in there again, Helen.'

'I hope so. My dialogue is good enough already.'

'Let's get you home.'

I put my arm around Helen. She seemed to lean into me for support. She was trembling, deeply, all over.

Jail doesn't do good things for people. It makes some people angry, some people crazy, some people despairing. Despite her bantering about dialogue, jail had simply and completely terrified Helen Thomas.

Lee Turgo was ready with tea and Berniece Able was pacing as fast and impatiently as her walker would let her when we arrived at Helen's duplex. Built in the late 1920s, the cozy apartment featured a keyhole-shaped proscenium between the living room and dining room, a cheery kitchen with homemade breakfast nook, and other amenities thought necessary at the time, such a built-in telephone grottos and laundry chutes.

'Oh, Lee' Helen cried. Lee's alpine complexion flushed as Helen rushed towards her. The two clung together for what seemed like an eternity, Lee in a flannel bathrobe, Helen in last night's evening gown. Helen seemed to gather strength from Lee's embrace. 'Just let me get out of these clothes and have a shower, would you?' She danced into the bedroom. After a moment's hesitation, Lee dashed after her.

I sat alone with Berniece Able. We listened to the clock for a while before I asked her, 'What made you think Carla stole your scrapbook?'

'I felt her take it out of my hand.'

I smiled. That's just what we like from a witness. Absolute certainty.

Berniece continued, 'After she became the house photographer for that ricket rag she got ruthless. Who does she give press coverage to? Waif lesbians under thirty!'

Just what we don't like from a witness. Lots of motive to believe the worst.

'Willie will be arriving any minute.' I said, and we sat in an exhausted silence until the doorbell rang.

Willie Rossini was a large, hunched over woman of sixty. She wore a gray flannel suit with a very pale pink silk blouse and bookish trifocals. She had a lot of lenses. She had seen a lot. And she had heard a lot of stories. But Willie Rossini was still willing to hear a lot more. She wore a big, black pearl in a modern setting on hands that were shockingly young and graceful.

Lee emerged from the bedroom in jogging pants and a sweatshirt. Helen, her wet ebony ringlets dampening the shoulders of a T-shirt, plopped herself down on the couch, curling her long legs in their heavy, black tights all the way up to her chest. I did the introductions. It was time to try and get all the facts straight. And to try to keep Helen out of jail. Those accused by the legal system need some kind of iron bridge over their back that will let the machine roll over them. Willie would construct that bridge out of wobbly facts and incorrect legal moves on the part of the law enforcement and justice system.

Helen went over the events of the evening. I prompted her to begin with the donation of her manuscripts to the Archive. Allen Boone had made an appointment to accept them shortly before the dinner. We went over the dinner and Helen's speech.

Helen supplied other facts about her literary background, the University classes she'd been teaching when she moved to town. She also volunteered that she had been arrested once before, but that the charges had been dropped. She'd been accused of assault with a deadly weapon – a Swiss Army knife, in fact, which Helen alleged she had been cleaning her nails with when a psycho ex-girlfriend came at her.

Willie probed gently with questions, and then finally asked the hard one. Had there been any romantic animosity between Tracy and Helen?

'It's practically public knowledge that Tracy was in love with Lee. There were some public scenes on an Olivia Cruise,' Helen explained quietly. I saw Willie's pencil pause over the paper. Nothing on her face changed. It wasn't the fact that Helen knew of the affair, it was the deliberately neutral way that Helen had said it.

'Right.' Willie looked over at her. 'I want to be absolutely clear with both of you. This is a murder charge. The DA's office will stop at nothing to make their charge stick. They are going to interview every person about what happened on the Olivia Cruise. So Lee, I have to ask you some hard questions. Do you want to answer them here in this room? Or should we talk privately.'

Lee looked into Helen's face. She took hold of her hand. 'I don't want any secrets from Helen, if that's what you mean.'

'Okay, Lee.' Willie paused imperceptibly. 'What happened on that cruise? Think very, very, carefully.'

We listened to the clock tick. Lee was choosing her words.

'I was on the cruise, partly as a Freebie. I had been taken on as the cruise chiropractor, but I was really just supervising three masseuses and a shiatsu therapist. Every now and then, if someone was in pain, I would make a diagnosis, perhaps start a course of treatment. It wasn't heavy work. I had a lot of time on my hands. And, well, Tracy Port came on to me pretty flagrantly.'

'Flagrantly?'

'Yes. She would move really close to me. At first I didn't understand what was happening. I thought maybe she was having some balance problems.'

'What did you do?'

'Nothing – at first.'

'Nothing?'

'Well, you know, I just sort of hoped it would go away.'

'When did this start?'

'In the beginning. Right at the start of the cruise.'

'And then?'

'She just seemed to keep making these passes in public. It was odd. I never felt her come on to me in private. Nothing ever happened – '

'You're sure about that, Lee?' Willie was leaning forward in her chair. 'Everyone on that cruise will be questioned, if someone saw something you say never happened, it's not going to look good for Helen.'

'Lee, honey.' Helen was smiling. 'I'd been on that endless book tour. If something happened, it happened. We've been together a long time, before and after that cruise. Whatever you did, it's not going to cause problems now. You'd better tell us what happened.' Lee took a deep breath.

'Okay. About mid-cruise, after a snorkeling trip, where, I have to say, I got quite a good view of Tracy's swimming talents, well, that night, I found her alone on the deck.'

'And?'

'I tried to kiss her.'

'What happened?'

'That's the hell of it. She wasn't interested. She wasn't interested at all! After all that flirting she just laughed and blew me off. After that I just thought, shit, the woman is schizo or something. I stayed *out of her way.*' Lee shook her head and ran her fingers through her hair. 'I never thought much about it again.'

'Okay. Thanks for that. Helen, I'll get back to you to discuss what happens next when I've had a chance to think things through. You won't be arraigned until Thursday. Keep your nose clean. Stay home. Don't talk to the press. Not the gay press. Not anybody. Change your phone number if necessary. Relax as much as possible. It's going to get worse before it gets better.'

'Do you think you can get Helen off?'

'There's a lot of things that add up too neatly and a lot of things that don't add up at all.' Willie looked through her trifocals at Helen. 'Helen,' the author sat up, returning the gaze of six pairs of blue eyes. 'Did you do it?'

'No.' Helen said. 'I didn't.'

'Okay.' Willie stood up. 'I am just beginning to build a case. I'll let you know when I come up with something significant.'

Helen nodded. Lee got up to show Willie out, her face a mass of worry. The boyish brow was getting its first creases. They would probably never go away.

'C'mon Emma,' Willie gestured to me. 'Let's go talk outside.' We walked together to our cars.

'Okay, Emma, I'm on the case and so are you. See as many people as you can, and let's collect as many motives for murdering Tracy from as many people as possible.'

'I'd like to put some of Rose Baynetta's techno-sleuths on to researching the history of Helen's necklace, the appraisals – '

'Yes, good. Oh, and one more thing, Emma. The anonymous bidder on Howard's place. I checked it out. It was Renquist Falkenberg.'

7:30 am. I buzzed by home for coffee and left a message on Rose's personal machine. Rose, it seemed, was still in bed. I went into Frances' office to look for old copies of the *Bay Times*. All these public figures. Suddenly, I hoped Frances was okay in Seattle. Didn't she need protection too? I looked at the desk top that might or might not have interested Fresca. There was the telephone number scribbled on the pad, the telephone number she always left, where I could reach her, in case of emergency.

It was too early in the day to call. But Tracy, after all, had been Frances' friend. Shouldn't I call Frances now? I picked up the phone and dialed.

After the ringing stopped I heard a synthetic voice: '*The number you have called is not in service. Please make sure you are dialing the correct number and try again. Thank you.*' I looked at the numbers inscribed precisely upon the pad. Engraved upon paper. The wrong number.

I pulled on jeans and a T-shirt, a windbreaker against the stiff early morning wind that came in the from the Bay. I was going to take a long walk this morning. To Red Dora's café. Red Dora's was always open. There were raves that ended at dawn, and a whole new theme party would begin around poached egg time.

I wanted to find a little punky girl, a woman who was pierced in all the most interesting places, and didn't mind showing you where. A freelance young lady who called herself Jesus and made a living with a polaroid camera. I clattered down the stairs.

'I don't want to know if you have an affair!' Frances had cried once, during our love-making. 'Promise you won't do it with anyone from around here!'

Now I realized why Frances didn't want to know if I had an affair. Because she didn't want to tell me about *hers*.

86

Chapter Nine

Red Dora's Bearded Lady Café

Somewhere it must be written that the children of capitalists will revolt by inventing a fashion which terrifies their elders. Every succeeding generation thinks they have discovered the final boundary of transgression, only to be horrified by the next wave of revolution in youthful appearance. Certain elements, particularly the twenty-nothings found at Red Dora's, discovered that multiple piercing easily did the trick as time marched towards the millennium.

Horrifying many a parent and passerby, they perforated their young bodies and dangled metal and jewels from every eyebrow, nostril, ear curve. They tattooed their necks, arms, wrists and feet. Bracelets and rings were inscribed on skin by artists whose craft was evolving to a high level of refinement. There was no shortage of living canvasses available, tattoos were the latest thing on young dyke hides in San Francisco.

Albert Camus said everyone is responsible for their own face by the time they are twenty-five. The girls at Dora's took this to heart and got busy at eighteen. It was a world away from the stockbrokers and dentists who had attended the Howard Blooming Lesbian and Gay Memorial Archive Gala Dinner. Thank God.

These girls hopped on their spray-painted and probably stolen mountain bikes and lounged around Red Dora's all day long, creating new poetry with their leather tongues and complicated affairs of the heart, which they referred to as 'the lesbian hairball'. It was in such a nest that I sought the multi-pierced Polaroid photographer who had taken the name Gurl Jesus.

All this piercing and permanent painting certainly put the women at Red Dora's out of the running for straight day jobs and mortgages. Having grown up watching the country being gutted by three Republican Administrations, these girls didn't look at the future too closely. It was never meant for them. They placed themselves outside the running and went on the rampage from time to time.

There were those lesbians with briefcases who dabbled in the occasional body adventure and hid a pierced nipple underneath the power suit at the board meeting. There were also those who removed their nose rings at dawn, before they went to the office. But these were not the women of Red Dora's.

At Red Dora's all the current conventions of beauty faded away and were replaced by outlandish acts of intention.

While the lesbian career women were still accenting the hollow of their cheekbones with clown-like blusher, women at Red Dora's had shaved their heads and got remarkable tattoos, mandalas of serpents chasing their own tails. Faces accented with silver, gold and tiny diamonds: Red Dora girls wore their wealth on their faces, in your face, and not stored in a lockbox or stock portfolio. The women at Red Dora's had become beautiful to me.

Red Dora's was surrounded by a war zone. It was a neighborhood of stray bullets. The walk across the street from the federal housing project, where a drive-by shooting was a monthly event, promised an adrenalin rush. I stayed on the far corner, and crossed twice, one more time than I needed to, even though it was far too early for gangsters.

Nevertheless, I thought about hitting the ground. I waited for the screams. because I'd heard them before on this street, at this intersection. I had seen the people running.

Bullets took out the occasional passerby, but they kept the rent low enough for a group of women as opposed to profit, and as unafraid of bullets, as the women of Red Dora's undoubtedly were.

I walked inside. Dora was busy cleaning off the tables made of manhole covers, suspended on legs of rebar. Dora did not have any piercing that I could see, but she did have a beard, a dark smudge underneath her chin. A long line of people whose clothes had seen much wear, stood impatiently in line, waiting for their cappuccinos, caffè lattes, peanut butter and jelly sandwiches, crunchberries, bagels and beer. Precious metals and gems flashed on them, like dewdrops on sleepy children. Children who slept in the gutter.

'Dora, you know Gurl Jesus?'

'What's this about?'

'Does she work here?'

'Could've.'

'Okay, clam on me Dora.'

'Who wants to know and why?'

'Let's go outside.'

'Well – ' The people in line shifted about uncomfortably. They were waiting for their caffeine fix.

'Brenda, will you take care of these folks?'

A listless blonde managed to disentangle herself from a rebar chair and sauntered behind the bar. Dora jerked her head towards what might be called a garden outside.

An illegal dog leaned against a group of stolen bicycles and twitched its ears.

Dora showed me over to a vinyl car seat which had been mended with duct tape. I balanced myself on the springs, barely contained behind the plastic material, and sent up a silent prayer against impalement.

'So Gurl Jesus – '

'That's Gurl actually, *Gurl*.'

'Whatever. Works here?'

'Who wants to know?'

'Listen, Dora, if Gurl has made a sudden disappearance – '

'I didn't say that.'

'But you're wondering why she didn't show up for work. The place looks a little short-handed today. Brenda looks like she could barely handle a damp sponge.'

'Maybe Gurl got sick.'

'You don't want to tell me, okay. But your friend with the Polaroid may be in trouble.'

'That's news?'

I heard something which could have been a car backfiring, a cherry bomb, a gunshot. It didn't matter to Dora.

'Where can I find her?'

'Emma, what's this all about?'

'I'm looking into the death – the murder – of Tracy Port.'

'That bitch!'

'Well, well. What's she done to you, Dora?'

'She owns a condo down the street. In the Victorian Mews. The neighborhood is poised for redevelopment. And they want us out. They started a petition once. But they failed miserably. We're doing our best to be ugly and in their faces.'

'There was a lot of animosity?'

'Oh yeah. Tracy Port, but it was that – that vile friend of hers – the southern destroyer – she was the biggest threat.'

'The southern destroyer? You mean Deborah Dunton?'

'Yeah. She owns a unit up there, and a seat on every board in town. Live and let live is not her motto. She came before three separate neighborhood commissions to protest our liquor license. You know, the only parties worth attending are her two-hundred-dollar-benefits.'

'She was on the library board. The board that hired Tracy.'

'Now Tracy's dead,' Dora mused. 'Who did us the favor?'

'I don't know. That's what I'm trying to find out. Gurl Jesus was there.'

'She's no murderer.'

'But people with cameras at the scene of the crime are always of interest.'

Dora whistled. 'So they might be – ' she said slowly.

'So where is Gurl Jesus?'

Dora looked at me, shut her lips firmly and said nothing.

'I'm not working for the cops. I'm working to clear Helen Thomas.'

'So?'

'So, maybe in the spirit of misplaced Sisterhood – '

'Sorry, I have no idea where I left it.'

'How about saving Gurl Jesus' ass?'

'You really think she's in danger?'

'I start thinking that. Especially as her friends are being a little too cagey about where she's at. There is a murderer on the loose. And Gurl Jesus had a camera at the scene of the crime.'

'Hmm.' Dora thought about it.

'Where does she live, Dora?'

'That doesn't matter anymore.'

'Why?'

'She called this morning. Said she was quitting.'

'Short notice.'

Dora shrugged. The concept of *notice* was far beyond the realm of Red Dora's existence.

'So why? What reason did she give you?'

'A lot of people here like to take off suddenly. Maybe Gurl is one of them.'

'Only the day after a murder it looks a little funny.'

'Everything looks funny to me here.'

'You won't be laughing if she turns up dead.'

Dora had the grace to look faintly wounded.

'So what did she say? Called this morning, said she's quitting work, splitting town . . .'

'Something like that. Said she'd stumbled on to something good, was going to split the country for a while. She was pretty excited.'

'And so where can I find her?'

Dora was silent.

'Did she have a last errand or two, before she left, or anything?'

'Had to pick up her paycheck. Came by earlier.'

'And then where'd she go?'

Silence.

And then it struck me. What do girls of Red Dora's, girls with a big life change coming up, girls with a little extra cash and the road on their minds *do*?

'Is she at The Gambit, Dora?'

Dora said nothing. 'I didn't tell you that.'

'Give me a name, Dora.'

Dora thought about it. We both thought about it. Gurl Jesus had been at the scene of a murder. Gurl Jesus had a camera. Suddenly being on to something good could also mean big trouble.

'Thad,' Dora said.

That was all she needed to say. Within minutes I was out the door, walking quickly out of shooting range of the projects, and watching the property values go up and up as I walked the long incline towards the Castro Village.

Garbage gave way to gardenias. Shiny brass knobs and mailbox plates twinkled in the morning sunlight. Ah, the Castro, where The Gambit, the premier piercing palace of San Francisco was located; where one Thad worked and had probably worked on Gurl Jesus more than once. Piercing was a highly personal, ritualized experience, and I knew that people liked to return to their original operators.

Being Sunday, there was a huge line in front of the place. Getting pierced was a Sunday morning kind of thing to do, I realized as I made my way upstairs into the lobby.

Picture posters of pierced genitalia, stretched and pulled in various directions like strange, fleshy parachutes, lined the walls. I avoided looking at them, and perused the personnel who inflicted such pain upon their clients in the name of beauty. Dressed entirely in black, wearing a turtleneck and velvet slippers, a piercer was showing a customer

92

the latest in Prince Alberts. There was no way I was going to stand in line.

Of the three salespeople, only one was male. A trimmed goatee was accented by two silver studs threaded through his lower lip. Both eyebrows had been penetrated, and the series of loops looked like a shower curtain over watery blue eyes. The salesman was busy helping another customer.

'A zircon can look just as good.'

'Are you sure?'

'Well, nobody could tell unless – '

'My boyfriend's a jeweler – '

'Well, honey, what are you doing in *here*?'

'He has to get used to the idea first. Then I'll get him to do a diamond for me.'

'So you'll take the zircon?'

'Yes.'

'Okay, you just sign this release form – '

'Excuse me,' I cut in. The blue eyes didn't look my way, but his voice said, 'You'll have to wait your turn.'

'But I just need some information.'

'Like I said, you'll have to wait your turn.'

'Does someone named Thad work here?'

'He's busy.' The man's lips clamped shut.

'Is his client a woman named Gurl Jesus?'

'I can't divulge the names of *clients*.' Irritated.

'What if they are in grave danger?'

'I only do body work here, dear, nothing lethal. I'm really busy, now if *you'll just wait your turn*.'

'Can I get this inserted now?' The woman elbowed her way in front of me. She was holding the zircon up to her dark skin, the fold between flesh and nose. It sparkled in anticipation and she smiled.

'Yes, just go into, let's see, booth number three.' He directed her quickly away. 'I'll send Georgia in to see you.'

That done, the young man, ignoring the whole line of impatient customers, hissed at me, '*Who are you?*'

'A friend of Gurl Jesus. Emma Victor. I need – '

'Well we're terribly busy, I can't divulge the names of other customers.'

'Did Gurl Jesus give Thad a large tip for quick service?'

'I can't spend my time talking to you, I've got business to – ' Then what I'd said sunk in. I could see his mind working, mentally leafing through my wallet. In a sudden stage shout he said '*If you want your nose pierced –* '

'Okay.'

'*What?*'

'You'll tell me about Gurl Jesus.' I whispered.

'Two hundred dollars.'

'One.'

'One-fifty.'

'One.'

Pause. 'Okay. One.' His stage whisper returned. That will be, let's see, the piercing, the stone, and would you like some cleanser? We recommend the cleanser. It's very sooth-ing. Helps protect against infection.'

'You better tell me about Gurl Jesus.'

He nodded at me.

'You will tell me about Gurl Jesus?'

'Yes.'

'By the way, no zirconium. I want this, *this* stud inserted.' I pointed to a diamond glittering on a black velvet back-drop. 'And the dish on Gurl.'

He brought out a pair of needlenose pliers. 'I have to bend the wire so that it curls a little bit on the end. Like these.' He pointed to the black velvet case where gems on the end of corkscrew wires glittered. 'The curling end keeps it in your nose; you don't want a backing inside your nose. This is the way nose studs are always inserted.' He held it up for my inspection and I nodded. 'That's one hundred and thirty-five dollars, will that be cash or credit card?'

I brought out the plastic.

'Right this way, Miss.' He glided along the tiled floor into the back on the silent pads of velvet slippers. 'By the way, I'm Thad.'

'Oh, *you're* Thad.' But he had stopped in front of one of a series of booths separated by purple velvet curtains which did not fall quite to the floor. I dropped a quarter on the carpet and looked quickly under all the curtains. I did not see the construction boots or tattered tights of Gurl Jesus anywhere. There was a pair of high heels, Bass Wejuns opposite to one pair of velvet slippers. The cubicle next to me had only slippers. The other feet were not visible at all.

There was chamber music playing, maybe Mozart, and the interior was medical. The instrument sterilizer was burbling away, the leather examining table had white paper rolled out over it in a big sterile stripe. All this was meant to inspire confidence. All I wanted was Gurl Jesus' whereabouts, I didn't really care if I had my nose pierced or not. But I guessed it was good that I was in a sterile environment.

Everywhere was white. The white walls had built-in white cupboards and drawers. What did they pierce penises with? Thad opened the door of one of the cupboards. I knew when he looked inside I wouldn't want to see what was in there.

'*Is it going to hurt this time?*' A gruff but nervous voice rose from the cubicle next door.

'*Only the prick.*'

Prick. Lidocaine. I imagined the procedure that was taking place behind the velvet curtain next door, where someone was lying down.

'So can you tell me, did Gurl Jesus visit here this morning?' I asked him quietly.

'*Ouch!!! Fuck, that hurt!*' A cry came from next door. Thad ignored it.

'I always pierce Gurl Jesus when she comes in,' he said. 'Except when we're very busy, like today.'

'Do you know where she's living now?'

'No. Now just hold still.' He held my chin in his hand, turned a dentist's floodlight on to my face and examined the shape of my nose, the crevice where nose met cheek, the shape of my nostrils. There certainly was a lot of space to a face. He adjusted the lamp above him and a spear of light penetrated my eyes.

'That's bright!'

'All the better to pierce you by, my dear.' Then he brought out a ballpoint pen and touched it to my nose. He held up a silver hand so I could see the little blue spot where the diamond would come permanently to rest.

'No, back farther.'

'There.'

'Okay.'

Thad was coming towards me with what looked like a Flash Gordon radar gun. Except that there was a needle-sharp bayonet on the end of it. In his other hand he held what looked like a plastic drinking straw, a half inch in diameter.

'Wait a second. I'm not going through with this unless you give me some kind of lead,' I said. Thad held his fire. The diamond waited patiently on a sterile tray.

'*Did you feel that?*' from across the curtain.

'*No.*'

'*Good I'm going to do another one now.*'

'*Okay. Hurry will you?*'

'*Two down, four more to go –* ' I heard from over the curtain.

'Gurl Jesus, she must have a studio or something, somewhere.'

'Yeah, that's what I hear.'

'Okay, before you shoot me with that thing, tell me where – '

'*Only one more left –* ' said the voice on the other side.

'*Good! I gotta get –* '

And then I recognized that voice, the voice from the body that was getting one, two, three, no six holes pierced somewhere through it. But before I could get off the table Thad's silicone tube was up my nostril and his piercing gun was aimed at the side of my nose.

'*Don't move.*' he instructed.

'Okay, Gurl, get outta here,' he called over the curtain. '*Run!*'

He pushed the piercing gun next to my nose. 'Just hold still. Your eye isn't very far from here, you know.'

As far as I could remember, I had not seen anyone at Dora's with a pierced eye. I didn't think I wanted to be the first.

So I sat there while I heard who I was sure was Gurl Jesus get off the table, pull on her tattered tights, zip herself into a satin sheath. I heard the sound of construction boots running out the back door of The Gambit and clattering down a San Francisco wooden back stairway. Gurl Jesus, running away from information that just might save her. If my hunch was right. But my hunches, I thought, were not always right.

My next feeling was a nanosecond of incredible pain as a diamond was permanently inserted in the side of my nose.

Chapter Ten

Dark Nativity

I grabbed the beauty weapon out of Thad's hand as it retracted from my face, and ran out of the cubicle, past all the other purple curtains behind which other patrons were being pierced. At the back of the building I could hear the heavy construction boots of Gurl Jesus still running down what sounded like a very rickety wooden stairway. I followed the sound which led to a small deck overlooking a maze of gardens and fences, my hand heavy with the piercing gun.

Gurl Jesus was scrambling over redwood dividers, trampling orchid gardens, bearded iris beds, hybrid hydrangeas and all the things that gay boys grow in San Francisco. I followed the tattered back of the photographer as she ran an obstacle course of Florentine birdbaths, Gargoyle Grottos and Notre Dame knock-offs.

Gurl moved fast. Good thing too. It would be seconds before irate gardeners would be outside, shaking their fists and clucking at the state of their gladioli beds. Then they would shrug their shoulders and work off their frustration by building giant biceps at the gym. Ah, white gay male middle-class culture in San Francisco. I could see Gurl Jesus' biceps as she vaulted over a bed of bearded irises. A different kind of biceps, a different kind of culture altogether.

'Gurl – wait!' I called. But the only reply was the muted sound of Gurl Jesus' combat boots, torpedoing through pale pink tulips. She leapfrogged a stone lion, getting her tights caught in a page fence. They tore, leaving a black flag twisted in the wire but she never looked up. She gave no indication that she heard me. The kind of girl that never takes advice. Jesus.

'Gurl – stop! Please!'

She just kept going.

'Gurl, you're messing with rough trade. Gurl, don't deal with a – ' But I knew she wouldn't listen. She disappeared over a final fence and I never got to finish my sentence. I aimed the piercing gun and took a dry shot at the fence over which the young photographer had vaulted. She would come out somewhere on 18th Street, I figured. But I wasn't going to chase her.

I wasn't going to trample the things that gay boys grow. I was going to go out the front door with Gurl Jesus' address and save myself a lot of trouble. After all, I thought, holding the piercing gun in my hand, I could get it easily, by nailing Thad's balls to the wall.

He was right behind me, thinking he was being sneaky. I turned without warning and soon had the gun firmly lodged in the hollows between his thigh and crotch. There was a big artery there. He knew it and I knew it.

'This won't be a piercing, Thad. I could pull the trigger but nothing would come out the other side. It'd be a one way hole. And it would hurt.'

'Look – '

'Give me the address of her studio, Thad.'

'Your nose! Let me take a look at that piercing – '

'My vanity will get you nowhere. I'm pissed off, Thad, very pissed.'

'I'm shaking in my shoes,' he sneered.

'Good,' I said, pushing the gun deeper into his thigh. It wasn't the kind of body contact I longed for on a Sunday morning. The barrel of the gun was pressed deeply into Thad's groin now. It made an indentation in the coarse material his dungarees were made out of. His thigh was hard and I had to keep up a steady pressure to keep the gun in place. 'Don't think I wouldn't, Thad. I know you've got enough medical equipment in there to do a quick suture, or tourniquet, when I pop your artery. I know it wouldn't do any lasting damage. Just leave you with a little unexpected scarification. I just had the gun held to *my* nose Thad. Now I'm returning the favor. It's *your* turn.'

'I was just helping a friend – '

'Yeah, get herself in trouble.'

'What do you know?'

'I know I'm just about out of patience with you. And I wouldn't mind pulling the trigger. I wouldn't mind one bit. You going to tell me where she lives or shall we just make a few holes first, for practice?' I had his back up against the wall.

Thad's head was tipped back affording me a look at his five o'clock shadow and more arteries I could stick my gun into. His chin was up high in the air and he was licking his lips. Christ, he was enjoying this! Just my luck. A masochist.

'Talk to me, Thad,' I crooned and brought the gun up to his neck.

'Be my guest.'

'Tough guy, eh?'

'I've felt a lot of pain.'

'Not like you're going to feel when I call the police and tell them that you're shielding an accessory to murder.'

'You don't have anything on me.'

'But you could have an interesting time cooling your heels at the Hall of Justice, Thad. I heard piercings don't go over so well behind bars. I heard something about someone getting – '

'Yeah, okay, I heard that story too. You don't need to repeat it. If you want to find Gurl, go talk to her. Go to her Studio. South of Market.'

'Where?'

'Somewhere.'

'Where, Thad?' I pushed the gun near the carotid artery

100

of his neck. Would I pull the trigger? Actually, I wasn't sure. It was nice not being sure. It gave an edge to my voice.

'Talk.' I pressed the barrel of the gun into his neck. The little black prickles of his beard seemed to push out of his skin. I could see his vein throbbing.

'Somewhere near that wino park.'

'Street name, Thad. Number. You're on your way to jail if I don't find her.'

'Sumner Street. 540.'

'Keep your hand steady for the next customer, Thad.' I pulled the gun away from his neck.

He stood still for a moment. 'Well, I've got to hand it to you,' he murmured, massaging his neck. 'I've never seen anyone get up and run like that after a piercing – you and Gurl Jesus both,' Thad's eyebrow rings twitched in what passed for genuine admiration. I remembered the hole in my nose. Looking down over the curve of my cheek I could see the twinkle of a diamond, obscured by something darker, like blood. What was Thad saying? About my nose piercing?

'Sorry, you still have a little blood on your – ' he reached a hand out which I pushed away. 'Usually people need to lie down after being pierced, they see stars, or get all hot.'

Suddenly I *was* hot, and the stars I was seeing were burning bright white holes in my vision of Thad and the back deck of The Gambit. The ground. I could fall on the ground I thought and just in time remembered what kind of thought that was. It was all I could do to say, '540. Sumner. South of Market. Next to the wino park.'

I gave the boy his gun back and tore out through the front of the building past all the patient customers waiting to be pierced. 'Nice nose,' someone called out as I ran down the stairs. I touched the tiny diamond when I got out on to the street. My car was still at home. I hailed a taxi and gave the Sumner Street address. I would beat Gurl Jesus back to her pad, I thought, confidently: I would talk her out of doing what I thought she was going to do. But I would have had better luck raising Tracy Port from the dead.

The taxi let me off. South of Market, or SOMA, is San Francisco's SoHo where you can get a cappuccino and a panhandler on every corner. Watch where you step; it's a public toilet down here, ever since the city decided to stop building them. Don't let your gaze linger on the outlandish signs hanging over the streets. Plaster Cows, rainbows, discreet eateries with menus in Italian; this is the intersection of Ripple and Thunderbird. Don't look up, you could take a slide on something nasty.

Or you could move in and have a several thousand dollar monthly mortgage on some wanky designer hut that is just big enough to turn around in. But hip, very hip.

Sumner Alley had a few designer huts, and a row of ancient flat-faced wooden buildings, storefronts turned into the odd living space. Down the street the wino park featured a big mural of Mexican revolutionaries and provided homeless campers with a colorful, backdrop of a revolution that would never happen here.

A group of men, down on their luck, were warming their hands over a morning bonfire in a fifty gallon oil barrel. A few pieces rested on a curling section of sheet metal. Everybody looked sleepy, rubbing their eyes. It was nine thirty.

Gurl Jesus' studio was in a Victorian Row house. I walked up a wooden staircase and was stopped by the wire cage guarding the entryway. Someone had welded a metal plate on to the grill where seven doorbells had been installed. A cats cradle of wires hung out the back of the panel and extended into one of the doorframes, held in place by what else? Duct tape.

I looked at the lack of names on the doorbells. You had to know who was here to come calling. Maybe you even had to have a secret password. Or a pierced nose. A row of shiny bells connecting to tenuous but tenacious lives through a thin two-gauge wire. Seven bells. And one of them had a cross on it. Must be Gurl Jesus.

I rang the bell but no one answered. So Gurl Jesus wasn't home yet. Any minute now, I thought. Any minute I would see her, have a little polite conversation and perhaps save her life.

I waited and waited. I thought about Frances and where she might be and how she might or might not have left the wrong number by mistake. I thought about mistakes generally, mistakes that I had made in this relationship, ways I could have been a better person. Then I gave up on this fruitless line of rumination. I couldn't have been a better person; I was only the person that I was. I'd almost had a one night stand with someone, that's all. I didn't know if adultery would have been wonderful or a major disappointment. I didn't want to find out. But did Frances already know?

I didn't want to think about what it might have been like with Fresca's fingers inside me, when all I really wanted was Frances anywhere in the vicinity. My mate who was not dyslexic, a researcher who had always gotten her numbers straight. I wished to hell I hadn't lost her research notes.

I sat down on the stoop and watched the bums make brunch. The dumpster pizza was sizzling now, and someone had their finger inside a peanut butter jar, wiping the edge of the glass. A broken bottle of what might have been port was passed around. Salvation Army forks and some cracked china with silver edges I could see from where I was sitting. One man stood and did the honors, parceling out libations and cutting what was left of the pizza into equal slices, arranging it on a piece of chimney flashing and holding it over the fire to warm it up. The other men drank and stared in front of them, waiting for breakfast.

I looked up and down at the houses, jammed together, no spaces between them for the rain to fall and the weeds to grow. Where people lived in them, the wooden fronts were blinded by shades, levelors squeezed tight. There were no cars. No action. It was Sunday morning. San Francisco was sleeping in.

I looked again at the bells and counted the windows on the front of the building. The windows and apartments must extend far back into the lot to hold the population that the number of bells indicated. Had Gurl Jesus come and gone? Or was she at home hiding? Waiting for some secret signal? I buzzed her bell twice, stopped and buzzed again. I sat down some more until I was tired of sitting. I kept looking for Gurl Jesus to come around the corner. Down the street, past the bum brunch, waving hello, in her tattered tights. She'd be scared when she saw me, but she'd stop. She'd stop and she'd listen and she wouldn't do what she was going to do.

But Gurl Jesus never walked down that alley. I crossed the street and took a longer look at the flaking paint on the front of her block. On the right, down three stairs another cross was scratched over the top of the door. Let the Pharaoh pass this house. The first born, Gurl Jesus, would be safe. Just in case, she'd provided a sticker saying, 'I'm Pro-choice, and I RIOT!' on her door.

The basement apartment. It was so quiet on Sumner Alley. Not a happy, contented quiet. Or maybe that was my head playing interference. Frances was in Seattle and I had almost committed adultery. By my fault, my most grievous fault.

That's when I decided to break into Gurl's house. And it was a good thing I did. After that things would not be quiet on Sumner Alley for long.

There was a small window with textured glass next to the door. It was small, but still bigger than my hips. I put my fingertips under the top of the frame. Dried chips of putty rained on to my fingers. If the window wasn't open I could probably dismantle it.

I turned around. The bums were burning their fingers on the flashing, trying to get to their pizza slices. They didn't notice me. They had never looked my way.

With a quick push I had the window open, had jumped over the sill and was inside the dark cavern that was Gurl Jesus' studio. I shut the window carefully, the rotten edge of the wood meeting the sill quiet as a cat's paw. There was a moment when I wished I was a cat.

Gurl Jesus' studio was dark as the jungle, damp and moldy smelling, crowded with creatures and an odor that started a cold stream of sweat that ran from my armpits to my waist. I stepped into the chilled room. No heater in sight. Permanently cold.

The long, narrow room was a dank tunnel with not much light at the end of it. Between the light and myself was something evil, something I didn't want to find. My nose twitched involuntarily and I held on to my stomach. The hairs slowly began to raise on the back of my neck. There were overflowing ashtrays everywhere, brown Camel butts decisively tamped out over and over again. Ashtrays and the smell of cordite.

Between here and the light Gurl Jesus had the place packed. Broken bicycles were hanging from the ceiling and thousands of tiny polaroid photographs lined the walls, signatures, or graffiti all over them. She'd mounted three old Underwood typewriters on plywood and stuck them on the ceiling. A line of hubcaps, shiny shields from vehicles that Gurl had never driven, punctuated the wall. A file drawer stood open, two hangers jutted out of it. A Rolodex spine lay on the floor, an empty Ferris wheel, every single card torn out and scattered all around. Business cards of clients, of photography studios, were scattered over the concrete floor.

Two old Samsonite suitcases, satin linings torn out, lay open, belching more of the favorite ancient clothes that Gurl Jesus, and many others, had worn for years. Stacks of unmolested CDs were piled into plastic towers and I saw that tiny, expensive Bose speakers had been mounted in all the corners.

A group of gloomy, still figures congregated in the middle

of the mess. They were stooped over, as if avoiding the bicycles which might crash into them in the next earthquake. I came closer. There were farm animals – sheep, a camel – and men with presents. They gathered around an empty straw-filled cradle.

I realized then that Gurl had somehow ripped off an entire life-size nativity display. I could just see her approaching the lawn of a church around Christmas time. It would have been in the middle of the night with the help of a borrowed truck, and a few other Dora dykes. They'd have driven up to the church lawn and made off with the holy family in the middle of the night, then installed them glee-fully in Gurl's basement studio.

Three wise men held out offerings in plaster hands. Smack, Crank, Cocaine. Gurl Jesus had made her own gift suggestions in graffiti, across boxes meant to contain frank-incense and myrrh.

A life-size Virgin Mary looked adoringly at a Barbie Doll perched jauntily in her arms.

A sheep huddled by the empty cradle. Someone had put a brassiere on the top of its head. The little pointy, plaster ears were sticking out from either side of the circle-stitched cups. Cross your heart, I thought, noticing that the cloven feet of the animal were wet with something black and sticky. And it wasn't some joke of Gurl's.

I was the only person around to witness the smell of the cordite. Gurl's plaster family stared with plaster eyes at what could only have been blood. I walked through the statuary holding my breath. Past a particularly thick-looking wise man, a camel hunkered down on the studio floor, something like a cow bell around its neck.

There, huddled by the hoofs of the humped beast, was Gurl Jesus. The young photographer was still holding her Polaroid camera. She'd just had her final piercing. In the back.

Gurl Jesus' shrunken cardigan had been bought second hand, after someone had mistakenly washed it in the washing machine. Tight and furry, it clung to Gurl's back where in the middle, there had been a small explosion of flesh and blood. The knitting and purling were coming undone around the hole where gunpowder burns left edges of the yarn charred. The lower half of the sweater had soaked up a lot of blood. But most of what had been inside of Gurl Jesus had leaked all over the floor.

Her legs flopped out from under her dress, a broken doll in tattered tights, the soles of her construction boots never to touch the floor again. Gurl was turned towards the camel, one arm outstretched, as if to reach up and pet its muzzle. The flowered dress was joined together at the sides by safety pins which, in some poignant irony, still held.

I didn't think she'd been assaulted. Just cold bloodedly shot in the back. The outstretched arm, the camera in her hands. Had she been meaning to take a picture?

I came closer, avoiding the sticky mess, a field for footprints on the floor.

I put my finger on her pulse. Oh yes, Gurl Jesus was dead. Freshly dead. She was still warm. She'd died, perhaps just moments before I'd arrived. A back window looked out on to a garden of trash and calla lilies. It was open. The murderer gone.

I looked over Gurl Jesus' dress, at the legs that would no longer run, the pudgy fingers that wouldn't push the camera release, wouldn't light a Camel or curl up next to one. I didn't need to look at her face. I didn't want to look at her face. The creamy décolleté, the biceps.

I bent over and peered at the camera. One of those fancy Polaroids. I took out a handkerchief and opened the back cover. Empty of course. I clicked the latch shut and slid it back into her hand where a snake tattoo writhed, just to make me nervous.

Gurl Jesus had lived on the margins all her life. She was only at home out there. But the one time she ignored that and tried to make a profit she forgot to look behind her. Where someone had a gun.

I looked around the dark studio. Without turning on the lights, despite the scattered Rolodex, the tattered Samsonite lining, I knew the place hadn't been ransacked. No, Gurl Jesus had gone quite easily to her crucifixion. She had handed over the photo, counted the cash, turned around and the photo enthusiast had plugged her in the back.

By *my* fault? Gurl Jesus, why didn't you listen? Emma Victor, why weren't you smarter or faster? My grievous fault. Gurl Jesus dead and I was no nearer to keeping Helen Thomas out of jail. I peered around the apartment again.

Gurl Jesus' filing system appeared to be old briefcases and purses piled up along the wall, most, but not all of which had been turned over. Papers and rags, stuffed animals and oil-stained doilies littered the floor. I tripped over a bicycle chain and peered into the bathroom. Someone had trashed that too; the semblance of a search, a swipe of the hand through the medicine cabinet.

There was a broken bottle of bath oil on the floor leaving a scent of jasmine which made me want to cry. A hypodermic needle and an empty glass bottle with a few meth crystals left in it lay on the tiles too. Gurl Jesus had been into crank.

Gurl Jesus was the kind of victim the cops loved to overlook. The half-hearted turnover of the apartment would convince them. Especially after they found the speed in the bathroom.

I went to the sink. An electrical water heating coil was neatly wound around itself. There had been no ceremonial tea drinking. No cookies. Just a bullet in the back.

I walked through the religious crowd and stared at the young woman on the floor in front of them, the brown stains on her fingers, the tattoo of a rose climbing up her neck. Why didn't you stop, Gurl Jesus? There were so many things I had wanted to tell you.

Don't deal with those who've dished out death, Gurl Jesus; you can't get credit with a murderer. You just get yourself a little closer to death. Blackmailing a murderer is about the silliest thing you could ever do. But then, giving advice to dead people wasn't so high on the smart list either.

I lifted the hem of her skirt, my eyes traveling up the threadbare tights which bound her thighs. Gurl Jesus had been pierced six final times, through her labia.

The plaster figurines were silent. They seemed to lean over the unfortunate girl, worried parents, a plaster family that couldn't figure out where they'd failed. I stepped over Gurl's body, making sure not to leave any tracks. I went over to the window and wiped any prints off the sill. The bums were singing now. Had they seen anything? Would they tell if they had?

The murderer had been confident, with the Polaroid in one hand and a gun in the other. I wondered if they'd thought of the negatives. You couldn't make prints off the Polaroid negatives. They were throw-away pieces of chemical transference paper. But you might be able to read faces from them. And moments. I started searching through Gurl's garbage.

Eventually, underneath a finally discarded T-shirt, and a pair of sandals with every strap broken, were piles and piles of Polaroid negative images. The curling, chemically treated paper teased me with vague reverse prints that recorded a gala evening with hundreds, no, thousands of faces.

It was the Archive dinner, but in reverse. I searched through the faces, looking for the table that might have been us. For the moment the murderer did not want me to see.

What would be on the picture? I could hardly recognize anything. Allen's shirt would be green. And his face would be black. Renquist would be a creamy white, with chocolate teeth. Everybody had chocolate teeth. Thousands of teeth. Ripping into cod which even in negative was a colorless gray.

It would take me for ever to go through the negs. I picked up the curling leaves of coated paper and pushed them into a plastic bag. I turned and said a silent goodbye to the unfortunate thrill jockey. I crossed myself in some silly gesture that I thought Gurl might like, then I slipped out the window and was outside, behind the glass that hid the horrible nativity that spelled Gurl's end. I wiped the woodwork and the doorknob and even the little bell that I'd pressed. No one was looking.

I walked away from the bums and under the freeway underpass to Bryant Street. I found a pay phone, looked for some dimes and cried. It only took a few minutes.

I was four blocks from the Hall of Justice when I made the call. A pay phone is the only way to communicate with the police. They tape the calls now. It's a good idea to put something over the mouthpiece.

The 911 emergency number rang and rang and rang. No emergencies mattered *that* much in this city. Finally someone came on the other end of the line and I heard the beeping noises which meant we were being recorded. I spoke quickly.

I said that there was a young woman who was dead in her apartment, on 540 Sumner, a young woman who had been shot in the back. I said it was a good thing she was already dead. She could have bled to death waiting for 911 to answer. Then I hung up and called my own message machine which answered considerably faster.

I heard the screech of a rewinding voice. Somebody had wanted to reach me.

It was Rose Baynetta answering my call. She wanted me to come right away to the Howard Blooming Lesbian and Gay Memorial Archive.

110

Chapter Eleven

Preservation

The playful parody that was the Howard Blooming Lesbian and Gay Memorial Archive stuttered in the daylight. Without the rainbow lights, the backdrop of stars, both in the sky and on the ground, our Archive looked like any other mausoleum. A cold and dead repository, available for anyone who wanted to hold up a distant mirror, raising facts and feelings from the artifacts of time gone by.

I would have preferred to have gone home to examine the negatives filling the plastic bag which bumped at my side. But, coming from the scene of a murder, it seemed like a good idea to show up somewhere very public where I would be noticed. I walked into the big Reading Room, clear now of the Gala tables.

There was a log book at the doorway next to a smiling security guard. I signed the registry with the time. The last person before me had come in a half an hour ago so I fudged by a quarter hour, saying a silent Hail Mary for Gurl Jesus' funky soul, and a few prayers that my presence at that dank, dark den of murder would never be known.

I looked around a room as busy as Santa's workshop. Howard Blooming would have been proud. I thought about his papers safely locked up down in the vault. Secure in a box in a safe which required two keys. And no one had them both.

A melting pot of people were mending, reinforcing and supporting bindings at long library tables. An elderly gentleman was removing a piece of glass as brittle and fragile as his own hands, from an old print. An aquatint. He examined the print with a magnifying glass, finding something which made him smile. He started to slit the hinges away from the backing with a scalpel. His hands shook. He worked very slowly.

I was surrounded by ribbons fading, images fading, the weak ink of early nineteenth-century dyke America, fading, even as we worked to save them.

I looked around at the big mahogany tables, like ships on a sea of history, manned by dedicated sailors with white gloves who peered closely at photographs, books, picture frames and even an embroidered cushion.

'Paper cloth, animal skins, adhesives – archival collections contain a wide range of organic materials,' came a chirping voice. I turned to see Allen lecturing a group of eager would-be archivists. He saw me at the same time.

'Hi, honey, survive the dinner last night?' he called and then waved me over to be included in his lecture.

'Volunteers – trained volunteers – are saving original source material, that is, actual photographs, prints, letters and books, that document some aspect of a gay or lesbian life. It's not an easy job. The natural aging process means that molecular chains break down, or depolymerize. It's impossible to halt aging, but much can be done to control external factors that hasten the deterioration of papers and other materials. Temperature, humidity, light, pollution, biological agents, we've taken all factors into account within this building. We're the *ultimate* control queens here.'

The group gazed around the room. 'Now,' Allen continued. 'In case, *just* in case, after this tour of the totally glamorous world of the archivist you still want to consider volunteering, you can give your name to Connie over there.'

Connie, a biker dyke in black leather, grinned warmly at the new recruits.

'I'll give you a bit more of a personal tour, Emma.' Allen took hold of my elbow and drew me away. He stopped behind the bony back of an elderly woman in a fuchsia pink jogging suit, her white hair twisted into a rigid French roll at the back of her head. Shriveled fingers with magenta nails twisted a band of linen tape from around a scrapbook. The outer boards fell open and revealed pages of yellowing photographs within frames of black paper.

'This is the collection of Marlene Higgins. The journalist,' he whispered. 'The estate turned over all her papers to us. She was a lesbian who won medals as an ambulance driver in World War II before she started writing for the *San Francisco Call*. Unfortunately, the medals were stored with her papers and have caused a great deal of distortion to some of the documents. And the adhesives.'

'What about them?'

'Oh, Emma, scrapbooks seem to be virtual catalogues for every known adhesive. They break down over time, lose their tackiness, permanently stain documents and initiate harmful chemical reaction. They say,' he eyed the album covetously, 'they say that Marlene was good friends with *Eleanor*,' he whispered suggestively.

'*Eleanor?* You mean Eleanor *Roosevelt?*'

'Yes! And *Lorena*. This is her scrapbook.' He pulled back and pointed.

The elderly woman, her skin as frail as the onion paper which rested between the photos, was examining the ancient album. Heavy black paper had been cut out to form arched mats which had a thin, white brushstroke around the edges and bordered each of the photos. I tiptoed forward, held my breath and peered over the shoulder of the preservationist.

Within one of the frames was a typical vacation picture with middle-aged women in 1940s bathing suits, the heavy elastic fabric, like girdles, pulled well down over their thighs. Their expressions carefree, these laughing, middle-aged people knew how to have a good time. Vacation photos. Water and sand, rocks and women with their arms slung casually about each other's shoulders. Four stocky women and one very thin woman with straight hair and thin, deter-

113

mined lips. A photo that could be anywhere, in any photograph album in the United States. Almost.

'Is that –?'

Allen nodded. 'Yes,' he hissed gleefully, 'that's *Greta Garbo*! With Mercedes D'Acosta on their Silver Lake honeymoon! And Marlene Higgins and her girlfriend Jo, who was some kind of oil heiress. Her name pops up everywhere. Marlene and Jo knew all the movie stars and the politicians.'

'Is there really a photo of Eleanor Roosevelt in the book?'

'I don't know! She won't let me look.' Allen lowered his voice even more. 'She can't hear very well, but I have to be careful.' The woman sat transfixed, staring at each photo for long moments, taking in the past, as if the photos were a world more real than the present.

'So who is she?'

'That's Jo! Marlene Higgins' girlfriend. She didn't want anyone else touching the pictures. She's considering having them sealed. Look at her, over ninety, walks two miles a day and is determinedly in the closet. I can't complain, I mean, she *is* donating the materials. She has some sense of posterity, of the importance of our history. I mean, how could you live in San Francisco and *not*?'

'Oh, you could, you could.' I thought about the occasional closet cases I knew. 'By the way, Allen, do you have many sealed documents?'

'Well, funny you should ask. There's already something in the vault that *we* don't even know about. Or who has the keys!' He raised his eyebrows conspiratorially. I kept my face carefully blank.

'Well, we're all in a state of shock here, as you can *imagine*.' he continued. 'Tracy's death is the only topic this morning. And, of course, we've already started on the Tracy Port collection.' He led me to what was apparently the temporary Tracy Port Memorial, or at least, a sketch of what it was to be. I shuddered as I looked at a long table loaded with flowers and messages and a large picture of Tracy who had unfortunately chosen a garish shade of blue eyeshadow for the photo session. A lot of lilies stood guard on either side of the silver-plated frame.

Tracy Port grinned from ear to ear behind a thin sheet of glass, as if no one had poisoned her potatoes, or done a bad make-up job on her. Tracy grinned the way she had grinned at Frances. Grinned as if it was still her Archive.

I looked at that heart-shaped face, the chin that was nothing more than a little dab of fat below her lower lip. Weak chin. Strong eyes. Sculptured features, tight as the chiseled edges of a perfume bottle stopper.

But there was something different about Tracy Port. What was it? Just my imagination probably. Tracy was just a photo of a dead person with a big smile and bad make-up now.

I glanced down at the scraps of paper, tender messages to accompany Tracy on her journey to the other side. 'Tracy, we will miss you. Harold.' 'For Tracy, with love, Arthur.' 'I hope they catch the sucker that did this to you. Love, Frank.' Most of the messages were from men. 'Tracy, you made the Dewey Decimal System look simple, Ginger'. Now *there* was a comment.

'Who's Ginger?'

'A volunteer in the microfiche department.'

'Working today?'

'No, we don't have a full staff on Sunday – even the volunteers like a day of rest, Emma. We're going to miss Tracy. She was a marvelous book and paper conservator. And that's a rare thing these days.'

'What do you mean?'

'Well, Emma, every year the educational system in this country creates thousands of attorneys, doctors, architects – I mean, *thousands*, and on the average, about *thirty* new art, book and paper conservators. While the *other* professionals are litigating, cutting, suturing and building – there aren't enough professionals to conserve the artifactually significant properties of our culture! Tracy wasn't an easy person, but she sure knew how to preserve paper!'

'How were staff relations?'

'Oh, ha, ha, ha!' Allen laughed. 'Tracy wasn't easy, as I said. You know, she issued a lot of orders through me. "Tracy believes this." Tell them "That's Tracy's view". When Tracy spoke it was excathedra.'

'Would you say she enjoyed being Executive Director?'

'This Archive was her life. She saw the Archive as the unique and extraordinary opportunity it is. But at the same time she wasn't great at community relations. She was always saying, "don't do anything to embarrass the Archive." She wasn't always kind to biker dykes who volunteered.'

'Would you say she made enemies?'

'In a non-profit organization this size? With the amount of work she had to do? Fundraising, administration, archival work. She wasn't always the *nicest* person. I'm *sure* she made enemies. But she got the job done. And, *she knew how to preserve paper.*'

'Emma! Where have you *been?*' Our conversation was interrupted by Rose Baynetta.

'Allen's been showing me around.' But Rose had no time to be polite. She pulled me rudely by the elbow towards the back of the room. Allen winked at me as I walked quickly to keep up with Rose's chair.

She led me back to a number of booths which bore an unsettling resemblance to the piercing cubicles at The Gambit, except that these had hard doors on them. Thin stripes of light went off and on and on and off in a steady flickering rhythm as a myriad of documents were photographed.

'So, how's it looking for Helen?' she hissed.

'Willie's agreed to defend her. There's a lot of work to do. Some of which I wanted to talk to you about. There's an opportunity for some sub-contracting here. We're talking print research, a few interviews. Historical stuff.'

'Hmm, esoteric,' Rose snorted. 'But I'll be glad to do what I can. Helen Thomas is no killer.'

'What makes you say that?'

'Oh, you know, I just feel that she isn't.'

'Look, Rose, I have to talk to you.'

I told Rose about finding Gurl Jesus dead. Her face didn't move. I told her about the people on the roof of my house. I mentioned Fresca, but not her .22. Some things weren't relevant. Yet. I told her I might have a special assignment for her.

'Emma, look here,' Rose said quietly. 'I want you to see something.' She went over to the microfiche machine and put a picture into focus. 'I'm here putting in my volunteer hours at the Archive and I've chanced – '

'Chanced?'

'Chance is always my friend, Emma. You know that,' Rose smiled and winked. 'I've got *all* the papers of Rudolph Sharpe here.'

I looked around the cubicle.

In its center a planetary camera towered over a newspaper column. Non-reflective dividers eliminated problems with ambient and stray light sources. Carefully lining up for the photographic process were a series of folders, books and archival acid-free boxes. The complete papers of Rudolph Sharpe, no doubt. Rose stopped in front of the camera and adjusted the lens. 'This system is capable of high resolution, we can shrink everything way, way, down. How many articles can be written on the head of a pin, Emma? Let's find out.' She reached down and cleaned the lens with an optical cloth. 'We got the microfiche equipment from a whole range of businesses that are no longer using that system. They're all going digital now. We don't have access to that kind of equipment, but frankly, I prefer microfiche. If you get the proper focus it's just as good as digital. Thirty-five millimeter, first generation, silver gelatin, polyester-based negative roll microfilm. Just as good as any scanner, stored properly of course. Rudolph Sharpe's papers saved for eternity. Or close enough.'

Rudolph Sharpe had been one of the first openly gay reporters in San Francisco, and in the United States. He followed in Marlene Higgins' footsteps, but with the closet door wide open. He was also the person who covered the Howard Blooming assassination and the subsequent arrest, conviction and the staggeringly light sentencing of Jeb Flynne. I saw that on the top of the pile of papers were yellowed news clippings of the riot after Flynne's light sentence had been announced.

As I stared into the half-tone dots of the photo I was transported into that night of rage. I heard the angry chants at bonfires, the gasoline tanks of cop cars exploding like cherry bombs. Flames broke glass. I remembered the community with a broken heart. Rudolph Sharpe had covered the riot well, even though his bosses were initially worried that his reporting would be biased.

When Rudolph Sharpe had started his career in journalism, women were relegated to society columns and cooking, African Americans to the sports pages and gays firmly in the closet wherever they wrote. Rudolph had been one of the many minority journalists who had successfully challenged those assumptions. Times had changed a lot in the newspaper business and people like him had a lot to do with it. When Rudolph died of AIDS all his colleagues, straight, gay, black, white, Asian, mourned his passing.

'I'm sure it was an accident that you got to 'fiche Rudolph's papers, Rose.'

'Not really, Emma.' Rose was winking again. 'I made sure it was me. They must be one of the most important acquisitions next to the final papers of Howard Blooming. By the way, Emma, where are *those* papers?'

'Safe. Sealed. And not to be photographed.'

'Oh, come on, Emma. Those documents belong to all of us.'

'But that wasn't what Howard wanted, Rose.'

'Tragic.' Rose directed my attention to the camera. 'I have to keep working, Emma. This is incredibly time-consuming. But worth it. Really worth it. Look – ' She lowered the lens of the camera and focused on a piece of newsprint. 'Did you know that Jeb Flynne made three trips to Washington before he shot Howard?'

'So?'

'And that he was active in college in the Students for Freedom movement before he was in the Army?'

'So?'

'Everyone knows that Students for Freedom was full of CIA. Half the people involved were there to spy on the other half.'

'Back in the days of narcs and Nixon paranoia, Rose.'

'Okay, sure. But Emma, look at this.'

I looked through the lens. I saw a picture of Jeb Flynne being arrested. There were any number of white male faces surrounding him in the hallway of a Sacramento County Courthouse.

'Yeah, okay I'm looking. A lotta guys taking a prisoner.'

'Look at the guy two paces behind Flynne.'

'The one without the necktie?'

'That's the one.'

'Yeah, I'm looking.'

'This.' Rose reached into her large leather handbag and pulled out a file which contained an old *Ramparts* magazine. I looked at the cover of the folded left-wing journal. A feature article on South America pointed out a number of CIA agents who were responsible for the overthrow of Salvador Allende in Chile.

'See!'

'See what?'

'It's the same guy.'

'Maybe.'

'What do you mean, *maybe?*'

'All these straight white guys look alike to me.'

'Emma, it's the *same guy.*'

'Still isn't pushing any buttons for me, Rose, sorry.'

'Listen, Emma,' Rose said. 'San Francisco isn't some little isolated *Tales of the City*, you know. There *are* international conspiracies. There are people that go undercover. *Here.* Moles! People who need to *disappear.* And Jeb Flynne was a CIA operative. I'm sure he was. While he was in college. He did demolition work for the Navy. He was set up to do the Blooming assassination. Then they whisked him off to some new location, with some new identity.'

'And then bought him a ticket to the Archive Dinner. Aw, Rose, I just don't believe conspiracy theories.'

'But – '

'Rose, Howard's assassination was twenty years ago. Jeb Flynne killed himself six years ago. There's a coroner's report. Do you know how many people would have to be in on a conspiracy that size? Do you know how unlikely it is that somebody, somewhere, hasn't gotten drunk, bragged to a friend, in the intervening twenty years? How do you think most murderers are caught? They *brag* about it, Rose. It's just human nature. Somebody has a hot story or an itchy conscience, somebody talks eventually.'

'And I want them to talk to me.'

'Rose – '

'Don't say it can't happen here, Emma. Lesbians and gays are the biggest political threat to the right wing that has ever existed. We are assimilating at a rate that is going to transform the gender culture in America. And it's the gender culture that keeps the patriarchy in place. When women and gays rise, beyond this backlash, we will rule!'

'Rose, listen to yourself'

'I think there's been a spy in the movement. I think Tracy might have been it.'

I looked at my friend carefully. Her hand rested casually on the counter. She looked calm and collected. She had access to any number of documents. After five years in the security business as a professional, Rose was interested in facts. Not fantasy.

Our little cubicle was silent.

'You don't believe me, do you?'

'It's just that I don't think that the world is that organized.'

'Just look at this, Emma – ' Rose bent her head under the machine. I held my breath as I saw an image coming into focus over her shoulder. A meeting of an old Socialist Workers' Union party meeting. Tired people sat around a wooden table with a lot of paper on it and didn't bother to smile.

'There, see that face?'

I moved my finger through the light. 'Tracy Port, right?'

'Yes, but look back there – '

'This smudge with two dark holes?'

Rose grumbled and played with the focus. It helped. I took in a sharp breath and looked over at my satisfied friend. I had met the other member of the Socialist Workers' Cell before. In a Sacramento parking lot. Tracy's comrade had been none other than Laurie Leiss.

'The revolution was different in the seventies.'

'Yeah, people killed people and blew up buildings. Tracy was a mole, Emma. Why do you think Laurie Leiss suddenly disappeared off the face of the earth? Tracy blew the whistle on her! There was always something strange about Tracy, and has been all along. Everyone said so. She was a queer sort of queen! Think of all the damage she could have done here at the Archive. Think of all the things she could have destroyed.'

I thought about it. I thought about pictures of Eleanor Roosevelt. And Greta Garbo. 'Come on, Rose. Is this stuff dangerous enough for the CIA to destroy it? Even if Eleanor *had* been First Lady, that was fifty some years ago!' I tried to put the Howard Blooming papers out of my mind. How I'd almost handed them directly over to Tracy.

But surely the whole thing was ludicrous!

'I get it. Tracy was a secret agent and Frances was her consort! After all, Frances has disappeared.'

121

'Disappeared! What are you talking about?'

'She left me in an incorrect contact number in Seattle. I don't believe it was a mistake.'

'Frances adores you!'

'Yeah. And I'm starting to wonder if she doesn't adore somebody else too.'

'You're paranoid, Emma.'

'And so are you. The CIA and Jeb Flynne. Tracy a mole? *Nobody* liked her, Rose. There are more than a few motives lying around.'

'It's true,' Rose sniffed. 'Then there's Renquist Falkenberg.'

'I thought they were big buddies?'

'Tracy supported Renquist's rival for State Assembly.'

'Joshua Haneman?'

'Yes!'

'But he's straight!'

'Tracy said he had a better voting record on gay rights. Renquist isn't exactly your radical fairy you know. Then there's that funky Fresca of yours. You haven't said how she was, Emma.' Rose's eyes held strictly pornographic images.

'Well, for a start, she isn't called Fresca Alcazon.' Rose composed her face carefully. I could see her getting ready for a document search. 'She has a driver's license in the name of Eleanor DeWade. Born August 14, 1968.' I gave Rose the number that I had found on Fresca's driver's license. Rose was already shuffling papers, eager to get out and on to the case. But before she called the office I told her I would need more, a lot more than that document search. Rose could handle all kinds of firearms. And, if necessary, she'd be willing to do major damage.

I walked home, letting the occasional Sunday bus pass me by. Happy couples drifted through garage sales, crowds of people came out of churches, a federal agent with a walkie talkie pulled away from the block where our house was.

I imagined the crime scene investigators going over Gurl

Jesus' apartment. Going over Gurl Jesus. I shuddered. I'd sat in on enough coroners' conversations to know their sense of humor. I wouldn't want to be present at the examination of the pierced and engraved body of Gurl Jesus. She deserved a better end. She deserved no end at all.

The federal agent turned the corner just as a helicopter floated overhead, taking over the tail.

Chapter Twelve
Bad Housekeeping

I grimaced up at the house, clutching the bags of negatives under my arm. The nuptial manor just didn't look the same. Would it be changed for ever by the moment I desired another woman, held her in my arms, heard her say 'I really like you, Emma. I really like you a lot, a lot, a lot.' The light would look a little colder, the shadows a little sharper, the curios and souvenirs mocking, revealing love for shallow sentimentality. The fog was rolling in early and I wasn't human today.

The third step up to the apartment squeaked in exactly the same spot with exactly the same tinny groan. Laura's lights were off upstairs but her car was in the driveway as it always was when she spent the night in. In the three years that we had been neighbors she'd spent the night out twice. It was hard not to notice. It was impossible to ask Laura about it. I looked forward to the day when her car was not so frequently in the driveway; it might do something for her humor.

I opened the door with the key which fit in the lock as it always did, tumblers rolling over like an obedient puppy.

As the door opened the cats mewed and waved their tails, gray boas, feathers in the wind; then turned and showed me the tight pink buds of their assholes. Fluffy was never as hygienic as one would have liked. Friend split to the garden.

The rest, of course, was more different than I could imagine. And I would never have to imagine again, because there it was in front of me. Everybody's worst nightmare. And now it was mine. Our apartment was trashed.

An earthquake, a tornado, a hurricane, a poltergeist could not have more thoroughly rent our home. It was as if some evil wind had come through and turned the contents of our lives inside out; had searched out, with angry hands, every corner and crevice of the life Frances and I shared together. Dirty hands. And disappointed ones.

The upholstery of the couch had been slashed, stuffing and feathers released. The room was filled with drifting clumps of white cotton batting, which Fluffy and Friend had no doubt made use of. Our books, all our many, many books, had been leafed through. It could happen here. It had.

I strolled from room to room surveying the damage, feeling a strange laughter caught in my breast. In the kitchen someone had made a bigger mess than Frances could have created in a fifteen-course meal. Our *cucina* had been completely destroyed.

I felt dizzy looking at it, the kitchen. Its center had not held. It was a storm-tossed ship, with all the wrong hardware. Every cabinet door flapped open and had regurgitated its insides on to the floor. Cups, saucers, teapots and tureens were shards on the linoleum. The cupboard was bare, its tiniest crevices searched.

The back door drifted open. There were jimmy marks where they'd forced the lock. I ran my fingers over the raw place where the wood had been violated. Splinters. A few pieces on the floor. That door had been an easy piece of work.

I stuck my head outside and looked at the maze of gardens, at cats balancing on one paw, washing their faces, at my neighbor going out to check for slugs amongst her tomatoes.

'*Buenos días!*' I called.

'*Días!*'

'Anything – strange? *Raro?*'

'Huh? No, no! Everything *tranquilo*.'

'Great.' I smiled. Just great. Inside I surveyed a bigger mess than Frances had ever thought of making, and wondered about the mess our marriage might have become. I was alone with it. And with picking up the pieces. There was no phone number for Frances.

A gauzy wisp of fog floated through the sunlight and wrapped itself around me. You're just feeling sorry for yourself, Emma Victor. Sit down for a moment and think better thoughts.

The Lesbian and Gay Stonewall Riot, the Lesbian and Gay Civil Rights Act, the Lesbian and Gay Media, the Lesbian and Gay Telephone Company, the Lesbian and Gay *Time* Magazine. In the end, was it all going to be the same? Would community just be replaced by capitalism? Replicated in lavender. Would queer matter then? Would my marriage? Wasn't that why we had to preserve our history? Would anyone bother to read it? Would anyone ever read again? These were not the kind of thoughts that would spur me to action.

Back in the kitchen the refrigerator motor tried to keep up; its doors flung wide open, cooling the entire kitchen, my entire world. The refrigerator and freezer had been emptied and a new stew, unlike any other, and spiced with glass, combined on the floor. Frozen Yogurt, Split Pea Soup, the strange Green Tea Diet Ice Cream Frances had bought and of course had never eaten. The strange foods she was always bringing home! The filo dough for some baking project that she'd never gotten around to. Was that apple season two years ago? Three? Would there be another? I was melting into a sentimental puddle as sweet and sticky as the mess on the floor. I was also crying, another hormonal trick. My adrenalin should have been pumping, vaulting over those fences, after Gurl Jesus, after the intruder that had ruined our home. Who was I kidding? The home was already wrecked. I suddenly felt that I was looking at the physical manifestation of what had been happening between

126

Frances and I over the last months. Why hadn't I realized it before?

Sweet potatoes and leftover lasagna. A ribbon of yellow honey mustard dressing wound its way over a sesame bagel and combined with a quart of milk on the floor. A container of French vanilla non-fat yoghurt had been opened and dumped on top of the mess; it helds its shape and wobbled there like a fez. Every cereal box, spice jar and tea tin explored. Small places. Small enough for a key.

I stepped high over piles of trash that used to be books, food and furniture, the stuff of two lives. As I surveyed the damage from room to room it was small comfort that they had not found what they were looking for.

I heard footsteps upstairs. Familiar footsteps. Laura's footsteps. Time to call Laura. Almost. I didn't relish the interview. But there was no way around it now.

I went into the bathroom where the last plant of my harvest reclined, a fine female plant that Fresca hadn't quite managed to get down the toilet. There were still some buds. THC, the active ingredient in marijuana, is not water soluble. Someone could still get stoned from this baby bud.

I put the damp plant on the slanted back of the tub, rinsed her off, wrapped her in newspapers and found a plastic bag to put her in. Then I put the plastic bag underneath the bed in the guest room.

I picked up the phone in our time-honored neighborly tradition. We never rang the doorbell. Doorbells make cops nervous. They made us all nervous. We used the phone instead. We thought of it as polite. That's what the world was coming to. I called my neighbor.

'Hello?' the voice came from the bottom of a well where fifty thousand cigarettes had been punched out on a pair of battered vocal chords. 'Who is it?'

'Emma.'

'It better be good.'

'My place has been tossed.'

There was a long silence. I watched Fluffy chase a fly,

trapping it between the window and her claws. Impaled, its wings droned helplessly on the end of one of her long, curved nails.

'I'll be right down,' Laura said. But she wasn't happy about it.

I spent the rest of the time looking for clues and not touching anything. As far as I could tell there *were* no clues. All the debris, from the finest toothbrush bristle to the broken spine of Frances' *Lavoisier* was indelibly, personally, ours. Except for the bag of Gurl Jesus' negatives.

And there probably wouldn't be any fingerprints, either. Then I noticed the final detail of the search that really made my blood run cold. They had removed the electrical sockets from all the walls in the apartment. The guts hung out of each little square hole in the gypsum board. Laura was going to love this.

Laura trudged downstairs in her white cotton bathrobe with a monogrammed initial on her pocket and a narrow, mean look in her eyes. Laura's shoulder-length, chestnut-brown hair was tangled, a state I'd never seen it in. Usually she brushed a hundred strokes but my phone call had interrupted her morning ritual. On a Sunday at home Laura liked to lie in late.

Smoking had given Laura a lot of fine wrinkles around her eyes with which she could do the blinkless fuck-you stare for a remarkably long time. There would never be smile lines beside those lips on that face. Laura had a grim line of chatter and she didn't give much away. I would have to offer something first. That wasn't a problem. You don't lie to the cops. You just don't tell them everything. And if you're lucky they won't arrest you.

'You've got five minutes.' A fresh cigarette dangled from trembling fingers and every now and then Laura brought it up to her mouth, sucked at it and blew a long thin line of smoke at me. I saw the look in her eye as she surveyed the apartment. 'I'm listening,' she said.

128

'Trashed,' I started with the understatements.

Laura looked at me, narrowed those hazel eyes into little slits like my face was leaving a bad impression on her retinas. She looked around at the kitchen, sniffed and coughed. 'Bad housekeeping, Emma.' Laura hadn't brushed her teeth.

'You could say that,' I almost smiled. Laura moved closer into my face.

'Nose piercing.' She squinted at the diamond. 'Very boho, Emma. Maybe you'll get lucky and they'll invent nose putty.'

'About my apartment – '

'Okay, Emma, what's the story?' There was no fooling around with cops. Even if they were your neighbors. And that didn't make me want to recite any epics.

'I took an early walk this morning. I came home and found the kitchen looking like this. You hear anything?'

'Nope.' Laura wasn't looking at the mess on the middle of the kitchen floor. She was looking out the window. At my garden with the three big holes in it.

'Garden looks empty, Emma.'

'Yeah, well, that's beside the point. That's not what they were after. The plants were gone before they broke into the house.'

'I'm going upstairs to my Malt-O-Meal, Emma. I suggest you take up the habit. It's easier on the kitchen.' She turned around, the stocky form in the white monogrammed bathrobe ready to haul herself up the stairs.

'Laura, there's more here than meets the eye,' I started, but Laura had already begun her rant. 'I'm just glad it wasn't my place,' she was reciting. 'I'm glad someone didn't decide that *I* had a green thumb and decided to break into *my* apartment,' puff, puff. 'Find *my* gun. Some criminal running around with my Walther because my fucking house partner decided to grow weed on my property. That would really be fun to explain to my Lieutenant. Yeah, there's a lot more here than meets the eye, Emma. Like why I ever – '

'Stop worrying about your fucking *gun* for a second, would you?'

Laura was always worried about her gun. Cop houses frequently get burglarized for weapons. I knew just where Laura stashed hers, in her dirty laundry. The last place anyone would look. Except me when I'd been searching for a rag to clean up some spilt red wine at our last dinner party.

'I want to get a security system, okay?' Laura drawled. I could smell a house meeting coming on. It smelled like burning hemp. And no AIDS patients were going to breathe the smoke. Laura was sucking in her cheeks as she dragged extra tobacco into her lungs and turned her back.

'Laura, it wasn't about the plants,' I said to her back. 'I don't think any security system would have stopped this crowd. And I've never heard of anyone expecting to find several pounds of dried herb behind a wall socket, have you?'

That stopped her. Smoke drifted over the head of untamed hair. She turned around slowly, feet first, then swiveled her hefty torso until those green eyes made a direct hit. Interrogation technique.

'You want to tell me what's going on, Emma?'

'They were looking for something small, Laura.'

'Okay. You going to tell me what they were looking for, Emma? I don't have time to play games.'

'When I came home I heard footsteps on the roof. Then they stopped. You came home. I went out for a walk. At dawn.'

'From which we deduce – '

'Someone was watching the house, Laura. They started when your lights were still out, after I left the house. They finished the job fast. There must have been a number of them. They must have been pros.'

Laura thought it over. 'I'm listening, Emma.'

'How could they have done this without waking you up?'

'You said that. Okay. They were looking for something

small. Small enough to fit behind a wall socket. What were they looking for, Emma?'

'I had been given the errand of taking Howard Blooming's final papers to the archive. I was mugged after I picked them up from David Stimpson. It may or may not have been an attempt to steal Howard's papers. I went to the Archive dinner with the notes, sealed them in the vault myself and – ' I thought fast. I didn't fancy telling Laura about Fresca. 'I took the key. This morning I put the key in an envelope, took a long walk and mailed it to myself. The mail comes between nine and ten on Monday. I think that's what somebody wanted, Laura. That key.'

'And now they know you don't have it. Fine. All you have to do is clean up this mess and wait until Monday. You want a police escort to the mailbox?'

'Or do I want to turn the Howard Blooming Memorial papers over to the police?' I asked Laura and myself.

'They need to be in a safe place. Safer than where they are now.'

'I don't want the Feds in on this, Laura.'

'The Feds? What are you talking about?'

'Laura, do you think the CIA is in town?'

'You're pushing fantasy land here, Emma. You were mugged. You grow dope in your backyard and your house got tossed. That's all. You're making me nervous, Emma. I don't want to be nervous. I need my beauty sleep.' She stubbed her cigarette out in a broken saucer.

'Laura, I'm really serious about the CIA. There are rumors that Jeb Flynne – '

That stopped her. Now she was going to laugh at me. She did, but it wasn't a funny, ha-ha kind of laugh. It had the derisive, hardened tone of someone who found human nature, notably mine, amusing. 'I've heard enough conspiracy theories to write fifteen novels, Emma. All fiction. The human mind likes to organize things into patterns. That's ninety per cent of conspiracy theories. Twenty years and no hard witnesses that have talked about Jeb Flynne.

Somebody, on their deathbed, on their way to the top, or the bottom, would spill it. It's just conspiracy theory to fit into all your nice conceptions about who's running the world. *Nobody's* running the world, Emma, and that's the sad truth. I know. It's my job every day to steer a little piece of it. And every urban city in America is way out of alignment. I'm sorry your house got trashed, but don't let it feed your imagination.'

'The CIA spy unit Flynne was supposed to be a part of – '

'Rumor, Laura. He was just in a weekend officer's training college.'

'This looks like a professional job,' I waved my hands at the mess in front of me.

'So? Crooks are pros too. Jeb Flynne was an idiot with an agenda and an assault rifle. You grew illegal substances in the backyard, of which I hope you have not a trace left, by the way. Crooks, Emma. Crooks are very, very busy people. Especially when it comes to illegal substances. That's the simple and boring truth. I just wish you'd stop growing pot in our backyard. Emma, when your plants get that big your delphiniums just don't cover them up. While you're trying to make a lot of chemotherapy clients happy I've got a profession on the line.'

It was time for Laura to have another cigarette. Her fingers were twitching.

She bent down to pet the cat. She wasn't usually a cat-petting person. 'You know what they say about the difference between cats and dogs, Emma?'

'I'm not up for riddles today, Laura.'

'Cats don't visit you in jail, Emma.' Laura laughed. She was really tough this morning. And, as ever, observant. 'You have a message.' She had noticed the button flashing on my answering machine.

I reached through the litter to the light. I saw the illuminated number, '1'. I pressed the button and heard a message rewind. Laura hung around, just to make my morning. She lit another cigarette and leaned on the woodwork.

I listened to the screech of the backward voice. Frances, Frances, I hardly minded if Laura heard a message from Frances. It would probably make us all feel better. But when the tape clicked, it started to play back a voice I didn't need to hear.

Beep. *'Hi Emma, this is Fresca. I just wanted to say that I had a really nice time last night. And I'm really, really sorry about your plants.'* Fresca Alcazon's voice blatted into the silence between Officer Deleuse and myself. Christ, where was the volume knob? Over the horizon of her cheek, I saw Laura's lips curve into a smile and I had a hard time not shoving her out the door. But it was way too late. For that and a lot of other things.

'A really, really nice time,' Fresca continued. *'And I just want to say something – '*

Oh fabulous, I could see Laura's back just shaking with silent laughter as she gave Fluffy a long stroke. She didn't even *like* our cats.

Fresca was huskily burbling away and I could see Laura's ears stretching to catch the sounds. I found the volume knob and turned it down but it was too late. Fresca's message was still audible in the Sunday morning stillness of the Mission. Laura's hand drifted down Fluffy's neck past her collar.

'And one last thing,' Fresca went on. Interminably, in that sonorous sing-song voice, *'Why can lifting belly please me. A rose is a rose is a rose is a rose. Lifting belly can please me because it is an occupation I enjoy.'* There was the sound of two lips smacking together, the audio waves of a kiss and a click.

That did it. Laura was laughing out loud now. I could see her lungs filling with air, expanding the fine bleached cotton of her bathrobe, filling her ribcage with chortles which made their way past her lips, a nasty sound, like a car backfiring.

At least Laura had managed to startle the cat. Fluffy

reached out a claw and then it was my turn to smile as she drew a thin line across the fine skin on the top of Laura's hand which quickly filled with the Sergeant's blood. So much for calling the cops.

Chapter Thirteen

Cleaning and Sleep

It was a morning for waking up with a partner, for making sleepy love. Sexual response would be dull and sweet, like a lazy bee on a sunny afternoon, lounging on a petal, just remembering the taste of pollen. The taste of Frances.

It was a morning for reading the *Sunday New York Times* reading bits of columns out loud to each other. Making love again and falling asleep.

Instead I would be scouring the pages of the *Examiner* for news of Tracy Port's demise and scrubbing my kitchen floor. It was time for the chore of thinking and guessing, which might, just might, be facilitated by cleaning.

I found heavy duty trash bags, anonymous gray sacks, for everything that was broken and ruined. Rubber gloves and earth friendly cleaning compounds. A new mop and three bags of auto-mechanic rags. I'd had no time yet to look at the negatives. Gurl Jesus, murdered. Tracy, taken out. Laura was right. There was no order, just chaos. No conspiracy, just circumstance. Gurl Jesus was a speed freak and speed freaks get dead often enough. Meth heads, the busiest criminal in the business.

They kept the fraud department at the SFPD busy all the time. They could stay up later and think faster than any dope-free inspector trying to chase them on the telephones. Speed freaks, zooming along in the middle of the night. Not only did their brains work at a remarkable speed, but worse, they always thought their plans would work. Laura was right. There was no conspiracy, no CIA. Just someone who wanted to kill Tracy Port.

I could use a little speed right now, I thought, starting in the bedroom and hanging up all the clothes. My retro, sports and second-hand clothes. The dapper pair of Oxfords with the plaid shoelaces. Sweatpants and sleeveless silk shirts. Cut-off T-shirts and old handknit sweaters. Sweaters that Frances had knitted for me. One double breasted pinstriped suit with matching skirt for the fortunately few times I had to make an appearance in court. Gurl Jesus, I pray I didn't leave any fingerprints in your apartment.

Then there were Frances' dress-for-success clothes, the rows and rows of hangers with the little double clips on each rung, row after row of carefully hung jeans, slacks and skirts. There were the communal ski coats and bathrobes; I slipped hangers inside them all. I worked quickly, not thinking about the fingers that had turned every pocket inside out. There was a lot of change and small wads of paper on the floor. Everything horribly strange and familiar at the same time.

I slipped on my Walkman and a Deee-lite tape.

> *Dee-ee-ee-e-e pending on how you see a thing –*
> *The ship is free or now we're sinking*
> *Depending on how you see it*
> *You cage your mind or you free it*
> *The world divides or closely aligns*
> *Depending on how you see a thing –*
> *we're wasting time or we're in a moving line ...*

'Deee-lite-fully' drowning out the vacuum cleaner, I swept into the kitchen. Some strange collections of sounds competed with my jangling thoughts and won, distracting me from all the things, the many things that I said goodbye to as they went into bags. I began to feel clearer as I saw the linoleum emerge.

I looked at my watch. Just before noon. Everything was clean. But completely different. All of the cracked knickknacks gone. An empty refrigerator. Not much of our crockery left. I was tired. I was very, very tired. If Frances had thought that I liked a sparse house, she would be convinced when she came home from Seattle. If, indeed, she was in Seattle.

My feet took me to the front door where I'd left the bag of Gurl Jesus' negatives. I peered inside. A hundred curled squares of chemically coated paper like closed palms. But my fingers were tired, and my feet automatically took me upstairs and into the guest room.

I lay down on the counterpane bedspread and turned the bag upside down. The negatives fell out with a gentle rustle.

There was a foot, and a shot of the mural far behind the cleft of a clean-shaven chin. One group photo showed hundreds of black-faced men with identical white moustaches. Our table shouldn't be too hard to find.

I perused last night's strange events in reverse, my eyelids becoming heavy. Was that Helen talking to some people at a table? Before or after her speech? The negs had no numbers and no order anymore. But surely *that* was Carla Ribera's long curls falling down the middle of her back. There was shot after shot of unmistakable Mojos on the bulbous belly of Renquist Falkenberg, whose face was as white as the driven snow.

How many people were angry with Tracy because she made use of the Archive to further her own career? How many people had ambitions of becoming Director of the premier research source of lesbian and gay material in the world who would want her out of the way? Was Allen really as civic-minded as he seemed? And anybody who knew anything about the Lesbigay literary scene knew that Helen wore, or purported to wear, a necklace with a cyanide-filled crystal. Publicity, Rose had snorted, and Rose was herself beyond suspicion. Unless she was schizophrenic, and had become completely *un*screwed by Carla Ribera.

Would I become unscrewed, unglued without Frances?

Laura Deleuse was right. There's no order here. Only the carefully orchestrated chaos of my unconscious and the demise of the relationship with Frances. Somehow that was my fault too. My eyelids were heavy.

I had no home in San Francisco. I floated about the city, through clouds of pollution and was pulled into dark cave, Red Dora's Bearded Lady Café. I found a beautiful brown lady in the bathroom. She was shooting junk. The bathroom was painted with flowers, its pipes were big arms, strong arms, arms covered with flowers. There were no track marks on those arms. They were the arms of Deborah Dunton.

There was no way out, out of the flashing and spitting of blood that was suddenly coming from Fresca's arm, and her mouth. The room was small and getting smaller. Fresca, I realized, wasn't shooting up heroin. I had been mistaken.

Fresca was building a bomb and Deborah Dunton was giving her instructions. Deborah's words were visible and filled up the room with tiny print, diagrams, arrows and words which buzzed around my head. Like gnats. Like insects that would sting and bite. Wasps and yellow jackets that would keep my hand away from the bomb that Fresca was building, the bomb that was being made according to Deborah's instructions.

Time was ticking, throbbing to the rhythm of a Bronski Beat, beating with the rise and fall of the ruby at Fresca's neck and with the extended hand of Renquist Falkenberg who showed up at the last minute to garner votes. Larry Boznian was riding on his massive shoulders, painting scenes of the Last Judgement on the ceiling; he was working from the curled up negatives of Gurl Jesus. But he was painting the photographer herself. She dripped red plaster blood out of an exit hole in her brain. It was getting mighty Catholic, and mighty crowded in the toilet at Red Dora's. I was almost relieved when the explosion came and ripped me right out of my sleep.

I lay in the afternoon gloom on the hard bed. I was tired. The color behind my eyelids was gray. Fluffy jumped on the bed; I opened my eyes. Fluffy was gray. The ceiling was gray. The air I was breathing was gray.

The dream, a draught so potent, so real that when I woke up I found the world past my eyelids a dull echo where people were merely murdered and framed, an echo that wouldn't yield clues without a fight. I woke up knowing that sometimes the best of marriages can fail, that falling in love can happen any time, anywhere.

I stood up slowly and then bent down to explore the bottom of the bed. I found the little .22 pistol. I double-checked the barrel. I wiped it for prints and wrapped a paper towel around it and put it in a plastic bag with a zip-lock closing. I opened the freezer door and put it inside.

I called Rose, gave her a shopping list and set up an appointment, then I started putting little devices on the outside doorknobs and window sills. Hairs. Hansel and Gretel crumbs which no one could see except myself. It wasn't a security system, but it would do for now.

The phone rang. It was Renquist Falkenberg.

'Emma, we're planning a memorial for Tracy.'

That was fast. I heard someone in the background, the sounds of coffee, a late breakfast being made. 'That's nice,' I lied. It wasn't nice at all. I was tired of funerals. I had not been a friend of Tracy. But I could feel the dark purple mantle of responsibility landing on my shoulders. Renquist Falkenberg was putting it there.

'I'd really like you to be in on the planning. I'm meeting with Deborah at her apartment. She has two clients at eleven. Why don't we meet at her place at two o'clock?'

I answered in the affirmative. Deborah Dunton. It was time I paid her a little visit – on my own. I decided to arrive for the meeting early.

Chapter Fourteen

I Dream of Deborah

        Deborah Dunton lived and practiced the art of
living out of her penthouse at the Victoria Mews condo
complex. If the Castro Valley was Gaylandia, then the Victoria Mews was our Buckingham Palace. An exclusive den
of rabbit warrens decked out to look like a big Victorian
castle on the edge of the Mission and the Castro, Victoria
Mews was not immune to the local crime wave which swelled and overran the neighborhood from the public housing
project in Red Dora's backyard.

From a distance it was a strange, anachronistic sight.
Victorian turrets and towers were decked out in a style that,
as you came closer and closer, was more a Disneyland kind
of cuteness than a historical re-enactment.

The real nineteenth century wouldn't have had the tennis
courts, the underground gym with three squash courts and
weight room, the jacuzzi and the residence towers arranged
around a large triangular swimming pool. At least the tiles
weren't pink. Not yet. The residents had put in a petition.

This co-operative venture offered a lot to the single, professional, childless lesbians and gays who could afford to
buy property in the Bay Area. Supposed security and bay-
views. They could leave home in peace, their automatic
timers set to turn on the lights, to open and close the
curtains. Lawyers, doctors, doctors, lawyers, couples and
singles, Tracy Port and my former therapist, Deborah
Dunton. One pet allowed. A lot of bickering over the color

scheme of the garden. And a lot of hassle for Red Dora's café when Mews residents protested their wine and beer license.

It was one-fifteen. I had agreed to meet Renquist at two. I should just be able to fit in a chat with Deborah between her last appointment and our meeting with Renquist.

I walked up to the main front door. A super-dense vinyl, the stuff they make suitcases out of, and molded to look like distressed, antique wood, covered it and sometimes kept the bad people away. A well-heeled young man was just coming out. I smiled at him, as if I'd lived there for years, and slipped smoothly past him.

Although each apartment looked strictly anonymous, regulated by the homeowner's associations – no pictures in the halls, no hanging laundry from the window – I felt I knew every thread of carpet, every individual nick on the doorway of Deborah Dunton's house. I had stared at it hard enough as a client, while waiting with Frances, to have that particular kind of twentieth-century healing, therapy, practiced upon us. Deborah's outer door had a coded entry. You punched in the code and turned the knob. I still remembered the numbers.

One, two, three, four, who does Frances love the more? Five, seven, six, nine? Is her heart really mine? Zero. The electric bolt slid open and I entered the tiny hallway as I had done before, as a client. But now it would be my turn to ask the questions. And 'How do you feel about that?' wouldn't be one of them.

With the permission of the homeowners' association, Deborah Dunton had converted a quarter of the roof into a penthouse and established her practice there. Deborah's therapy was quiet. There would be no primal screams coming from her apartment. Just gentle sniffles and a few sobs and some counter-transference that made you feel really shitty later.

I entered the vestibule which was made over into a waiting room. My eyes adjusting to the dark mauve I heard the familiar whistling sound which came from a noise-making machine Deborah employed. Therapy muzak, a melodic, rhythmic whoosh, like the tape of a bad ventilation system. It was designed to cover up any embarrassing sniffles or cries. 'Shhhh,' it said.

There were lots of quiet prints of flowers in brass frames. I sat in one of the two matched chintz chairs and stared at the reassuring pattern of stripes woven into the maroon carpet at my feet. I listened to my nerves jangle. How many times had I sat in that chair, waiting, with Frances, trying to learn to talk about our relationship. '*Shhhh*,' counseled the noise machine.

Why could other people talk so easily about their feelings and not I? How did they do it? When emotions bubbled up inside of me they never took the form of words. Sometimes feelings took the form of music, of sex. Even food. But they never took the form of words. The best I ever did was pronounce boundary statements. I had a long way to go.

The door from the inner sanctum opened.

Four white tennis shoes came out on to the carpet. Stiff bleached white linen shorts with colorful tennis tops and tennis arms coming out of the sleeves. But the expression on these clients' faces were nothing alike and if there was anything they were going to do, it wasn't play tennis. '*Shhhh*,' counseled the noise machine.

'Thank you, Deborah,' a blonde said. The brunette didn't say anything. She was holding on tight, her face taut, to avoid melting on to the floor. She was devastated.

'Are you okay, Jane?' came the dulcet professional tones of Deborah Dunton.

'Of course I'm not okay,' Jane shouted. The noise machine didn't have a chance. 'My girlfriend just sprung on me that she's in love with someone else! What is it, you're too much of a coward to tell me to my face, one to one, is that it, huh?'

'That's exactly why I had to tell you *here*, honey,' the blonde said, 'in therapy; so I can feel safe, with Deborah!'

'Taking sides again, Deborah?'

'Emma! What are you doing here?' Deborah's face clouded and it took her a full two seconds to put the peaceful therapeutic smile back on. 'Jane, Meg, why don't you go home and do some of those honesty exercises – '

'Hey, why didn't she tell me about Sharon during last week's honesty exercise! Huh? You coward, Meg!' Jane cried.

'It would have saved you a hundred bucks,' I said from the sidelines.

'Emma, I don't need your wit.'

'You never did.' '*Shhhh*,' counseled the noise machine.

'Call me, Meg, Jane, if you need to, I'm always available for another emergency session.' Deborah was shoving them out the door.

'Yeah, and don't forget your checkbook,' I cracked but the door had closed with a sad finality. Dunton leaned against it, making me feel terribly trapped in her hallway. She was wearing an olive-green peasant dress of a thick linen which covered her slight frame in heavy folds. Dark red lipstick was slashed across her tiny lips. A little stripe of red raced across one on her front teeth, making her look like a fox that had been at the chickens.

'What's going on, Emma? Is there something I can help you with?'

'I just want to ask you a few questions.'

'Well you have a funny way of going about it. Are you trying to ruin my business, or what?'

'Sorry, I regressed.'

Deborah looked at me closely. 'Okay, let's talk about regression Emma. And aggression. A suitable topic, don't you think? But you'll have to wait, just for a moment. I have to attend to my notes.' Deborah disappeared behind the famous door of her therapy chamber. I watched the carpet for a while and wondered what kind of notes Deborah took. And why. I had ruminated enough for a few novels when Deborah reappeared.

The blood-red color had gone from her teeth and she had on a feverish version of her therapist smile. She wandered over towards me, the folds of her dress moving rhythmically. 'Couples' counseling.' She breathed the words into my face, and I realized she had been drinking. I could have lit her breath with a match. 'Oh Emma, sometimes I think I just function to take the rap for bad relationships!'

'Well, at least you're paid for it.'

'Too bad I don't have any friends left. Even *you* won't be friends with me after – by the way, how *are* you and Frances.'

'Deborah, I'm here investigating the murder of Tracy Port.'

'*Really?* Who's your client, Emma. Helen Thomas? Good luck. She's guilty, Emma. Guilty as *sin*.'

'A surprising judgement call from a therapist, Deborah. Listen, I just need answers to a few simple questions. You don't need to put a noose around Helen's neck or solve the world's problems.' Or drink whiskey.

'I'll try and restrain myself,' Deborah's mouth contorted into a very untherapeutic sneer as she showed me into her office. It hadn't changed a bit.

The child within was not only welcome, but forced out in a Caesarean section of the mind by Deborah's interior. The room was determinedly cheerful, each corner filled with the reminder of a sunny thought. Wreathes of dried flowers, nosegays of roses and willow twigs hung from the ceiling; framed mottos and paintings of goddesses surrounded Deborah's clients with their good humor. This surfeit of effort felt ultimately depressing even before you saw the toys.

An entire population of tiny figurines crowded together on a bookshelf that stretched from floor to ceiling. '*Shhhh*,' counseled the noise machine.

From Batman to Snow White and the Seven Dwarfs, the Hulk to Cinderella, little molded rubber figurines had multiplied on Deborah's bookshelf, an army ready for role playing. The idea was to identify with one of them and do some acting out with the small rubber dolls, rather than with your partner. It was a way to understand and maybe verbalize your feelings. It had just made me feel like an idiot.

During sessions my attention had always drifted to the titles on the spines of Deborah's library. There were books. Lots and lots of books. Had she read them all, I wondered?

The author of *Lesbians Who Love Too Much* looked at me directly. 'So what can I tell you, Emma?'

'I was wondering if you could shed a little bit of light on Tracy's last weeks.'

'I didn't really see Tracy much, as you know. Not after the cruise.'

'Did you notice anything different about her in the last weeks?'

'Why don't you ask Lee Turgo?' She said bitterly.

'What makes you think Lee Turgo was seeing Tracy?'

'It was obvious, Emma. I was there on that cruise when they got together. And Tracy was still in love with Lee, right up to the end.'

'How would you know that?'

'I know Tracy when she is in love, Emma, she was in love with me. Once.'

'And?'

'And – she whistled.'

'She *whistled?*'

'Listen Emma, Tracy lives – lived – right down the hall from me. It's not like our bathrooms are connected, but believe me, I know Tracy. I know that she was in love. Because she whistled when she was in love with me. There's part of me that is attuned to Tracy. No matter how mean, or deferential, or even rude Tracy's been, I know I touched –' Deborah allowed herself a few deep breaths, high octane breaths, and continued.

'I'd watched them flirting together on that cruise. Everybody on the boat knew Helen was on a book tour. And

145

who wouldn't take Tracy if they were given half a chance?'
I could think of plenty of people, but then I wasn't in love
with Tracy Port. 'Besides,' Deborah continued, 'if Tracy was
in love, it had to be with somebody married. It had to be.
It *had* to be Lee.'

'I'm not following you, Deborah.'

She said, with the kind of confidence only therapists can
have, 'There is so little justice in the world, Emma. I see
that all the time as a therapist. I see adults that are really
damaged children. Tracy had a very unhappy upbringing.
She had issues. Intimacy issues. Abuse issues. I believe Tracy
was severely traumatized as a child.'

'Why do you think Tracy had been abused as a child. Did
she ever tell you that?'

'She didn't have to. She kept many, many things to herself.
But I'm a therapist Emma. There are things that I know.
Tracy could only give of herself – sexually – when her lover
was a stranger. The first time was wonderful. Making love
with Tracy Port was the most intense experience of my life,
Emma. But she wanted to spill all that love and passion on
somebody who didn't care. When you start to care, she
cools off.' Deborah sniffed and her little foot drew a pattern
in the air. 'It's a common pattern. Not just for lesbians. For
the whole of society.'

Deborah turned to her bookshelf and picked up a molded
rubber figurine, Sleeping Beauty. 'In a way, Tracy was sleeping, and I, in my own egocentric way, thought I would be
able to wake her. But she moved on. On to Lee Turgo.'
Deborah's gaze was directed towards a rubber snake with
large fangs. 'A woman who was profoundly engaged with
someone else, and therefore fundamentally unavailable. At
some level, Lee would always remain apart from Tracy – a
stranger to her.'

'How long did you and Tracy live in the same building
Deborah?'

'*Shhhh*,' counseled the noise machine.

'You'll find out soon enough, Emma, and I don't mind

telling you. I made the down payment on Tracy's flat. It was when we were together. I also helped Tracy out with her last year's tuition at the School of Library Science. I don't have any regrets. Tracy was an excellent librarian. I voted for her as Executive Director for the Archive. It was a unanimous vote, by the way. Everyone on the Board thought that Tracy was the most qualified candidate. She had her problems with personal relationships, but she was one hell of an executive director.'

'About the down-payment on Tracy's flat. How much was it?'

'A hundred thousand.' She sniffed.

'A hundred thousand dollars?'

'She was paying it back, a thousand a month.'

'She could afford it once she was Executive Director of the Library.'

'That's not why I voted for her, Emma. You have such a suspicious mind.'

'It's my job.'

'Why don't you blame Helen Thomas? Tracy went around having hyperdramatic sex with all kinds of people. It's not exactly a life insurance policy.'

'Did Tracy have any?'

'Sex?'

'Life insurance.'

'Well, I may as well tell you. You'll find out anyway. Yes, Tracy had taken out life insurance. It was for the outstanding amount of the condo down-payment.'

'So she paid you back?'

'More than that, Emma, I not only have the down-payment returned to me, but I've inherited Tracy's condo as well. That is, if she hasn't changed her will.'

'Has she?'

'I don't know. I didn't keep track once we broke up. I received a copy of her life insurance policy as part of our agreement. But I didn't know about her will. I still don't. I imagine we'll find out once her safety deposit box is unsealed. The police were over in her apartment this morning, looking for clues.'

'Do you have a key, Deborah?'

'What makes you think I do?'

'It happens. You live in the same building. You were lovers. Aren't you on the Board of Directors of the Homeowners' Association?'

'Yes,' Deborah said slowly, her tongue licking her little red lips. She needed that whiskey. She needed it bad. She'd needed it for a long time. But that wasn't all. Deborah Dunton needed something she thought of as love. Badly.

'Well, do you have a pass key?' I asked.

There was a nice positive silence.

'I can find out from your bylaws, you know.'

'Ah – ah don't – ' There came that Southern accent again, every time Deborah got nervous.

'I just want to take a little look around, Deborah. The police have already been there. Let's see if there's any caution tape, if the door to her apartment is sealed or anything.'

Deborah paused long enough to give me the impression that she was thinking about it. Then she started to shake her head. I'd have to try some magic words.

'The relationship is going really shitty with Frances,' I confided. It was just the aperitif for Deborah's appetite.

'It isn't!' Then, 'I'm so sorry.'

'Really. It's just as you said, Deborah. I think Frances is tired of my intimacy issues.'

Deborah looked me up and down. She wasn't a stupid woman.

'You know, I just can't seem to talk, I don't have the words for things that other people have.' My performance was getting a little too real for comfort. But it was working. Deborah switched on her therapist gaze and knitted her eyebrows in a familiar way that had always made me want to shut up. This time it had to do the opposite. 'Feelings for me just don't have words, they're like colors. When I start to talk the colors go all muddy – '

'Emma, have you read my book?'

'No.' I tried to sound confessional.

'I'll go get a copy.' Deborah turned and smiled at me with the tiniest, most terrifying air of delight. 'And I'll bring the key to Tracy's apartment.' She hauled herself out of her chair with some difficulty. Her weak arms were no match for her drunken brain.

Deborah opened a door I have never seen her open before. It was the door to her personal apartment. The part she lived in. I peered around her back at a lot of pink walls and pastel accents, as she gripped the sides of the door-frame. The apartment was full, as I might have expected, of flowers. Deborah swayed slightly, like a small refrigerator with feet, trying to make it through the door.

I took the opportunity to find out just exactly what kind of notes Deborah liked to take on her clients. I went over to her filing cabinet. It was locked, but its keychain swung above it from a bulletin board. I opened that drawer of Deborah Dunton's with her own key. Inside it I found Frances' *Lesbo-Parthenogenesis* notes.

I pushed the drawer closed.

For a moment I sat down on the couch, the very spot where I had sat so many times with Frances. The experience receded, far away from me. There was something inside me that was turning numb. I stood up and followed Deborah Dunton into her private apartment. Inside I stopped short.

Chintz, needlepoint and hand-crocheted lace. And guns.

A plexiglass, locked wall cabinet full of guns.

Chapter Fifteen
Tracy's Terrain

Deborah's apartment had a basic twentieth-century open-floor plan. A corner kitchen with white Italian cabinets, built-in appliances in white. A white dishwasher, trash compactor, microwave, wall oven and stove top. Flowered chintz curtains were gathered on either side of a view of Twin Peaks which was already funneling a blanket of fog into the valley.

The counter was a bright egg-yolk yellow and there was a passthrough to a dining room where a circular table was covered in a primrose print and matching highly upholstered chairs circled around it, the covers held on by big, fluffy pink ribbons.

There was a long living room off to the right, an expanse of white carpet and lots of aqua wicker furniture. A small dark hallway led to what was undoubtedly a bedroom, where Deborah was probably having another pull for the road and searching for her keys.

I stood in the other dark hallway off the kitchen examining Deborah's gun collection. It was quite a little stash. For a therapist. Or a white supremacist.

Single shot muskets. Antique revolvers that looked beyond use. A shotgun with a carved mahogany handle, all in a plexiglass case with a wimpy lock that would be alarmingly easy to pick or pull off.

'Mah Daddy's,' Deborah said from behind my back, her Southern heritage revealing itself again. 'He left them to me. Quite a collection, wouldn't you say? You know how we Southerners are about our guns. And our whiskey. How 'bout it?' Deborah's breath was a confession that threatened to knock me off my feet.

'A little early in the day, Deborah – '

'Nonsense, come over and sit by me on the couch, Emma – '

Reports of women accosted by their male therapists were no longer surprising, but we lesbians were supposed to be above all that. Dream on. That gutter rolled all kinds of balls. Just less frequently. 'Let's talk and drink when we get back, okay Deborah?'

There was a smile deep in Deborah's eyes that rose to the surface a little too quickly for my peace of mind. She turned her back long enough to take an obvious swig from a hip flask that she had in her pocket. When she turned back to me her eyes were all hard and glittery, just like before. Then she went over and got a hardbound copy of *Lesbians Who Love Too Much*.

'I'll sign it later,' Deborah promised with a wink.

As we walked out into the hallway Deborah closed the door behind her, first pulling out the little button on the inside knob so we could get in again without the key. It was a practiced gesture. Something Deborah had done hundreds of times so she could roam the corridors of Victoria Mews. As we walked down the plush carpet, underneath the regulation sprinklers and fire extinguishers, Deborah became quieter and quieter.

Eventually, she murmured 'I have my ears tuned to this hallway, as you can imagine. Listening, still listening for Tracy. I'll probably be listening to this hallway for the rest of my life, Emma.'

'Twenty-seven steps!' she announced, wobbling slightly at the entrance to another apartment, identical to her own.

'I wasn't counting.' But I realized that Deborah *had* been. Maybe for years now. Lesbians Who Loved Too Much.

'Is there any other way into Tracy's apartment?'

'There's a service stairway.'

'Someone could come and go without being seen?'

'I guess so. The service stairwell serves six units.'

Deborah paused, her key in the lock. I sucked in a breath. Why did I imagine that there must be something terrible behind that door?

But the door opened on a Tracy Port I never could have imagined. A Tracy Port I might not have minded knowing. Soft green light filtered through seafoam shades. The walls had been papered in a satiny silken grasspaper, a silvery texture that was like a soft mattress for the eyes. My pupils slowly adjusted to the dim light. So quiet. So peaceful. Was there another Tracy Port, someone who was much more likable?

There were smokey green carpets underfoot, high ticket items stretching out on a blond finished floor in a long living room identical to the one that Deborah had, but so much classier. Tracy had chosen olive-green kitchen cabinets, black appliances and a bird's eye maple counter. It was almost austere.

The long living room was suffused with green, the blond accents continuing in the light gold reflected in built-in bookcases and coffee tables and a cozy spinet piano in the corner. The whole place was as neat and orderly as a bread and butter note.

Deborah was sniffling. I thought about the frilly fuss of her place and how she must have loved this haven of quiet just down the hall. Deborah had the cash, but Tracy had the taste, that much was clear. Part of that down-payment must have gone towards silken wallpaper and *Kazistan* carpets.

Had Tracy done Deborah for the down-payment? And then dumped her?

Deborah was walking around the center of the big living room, slipping slightly on the carpets which shifted under her weight on the slick floor. Waving her long arms,

Deborah seemed to be embracing the air of Tracy's apartment. And why not? It was hers now.

I looked at the carpets and the tracks across them. The tracks of professionals, the tracks of tears. Deborah had seated herself on the middle of a bamboo settee in the living room. Her fingers were walking through her hair, grabbing at tufts and pulling them. Deborah was getting a little scary.

I would start my search in the kitchen.

A librarian's kitchen. The rice and the bulgur and the beans might all have been in alphabetical order. Everything in tidy rows, glass jars, lids clamped on. I picked them up methodically and shook each one. Rice, beans and bulgur.

I looked in the refrigerator. Tracy liked food, good food. Eggplants with organic stickers. Pomodoro tomatoes. Some basil in a bag which had turned black and mushy. A protein drink. Had Tracy been worried about being too thin? You could never be too rich or too thin – an upper-class straight woman's motto. I looked in the garbage can. Recently emptied.

Everything indicated strict control. The rigid color scheme. Not a mismatched cup or saucer. Not a chipped memento, or an article stuck to the refrigerator. I checked all the cupboards quickly. The freezer was full of ice cream. Gallons of cherry Garcia competing with Health Bar crunch. Dairy.

'Say, Deborah, about Tracy's allergies – ' I said, but stopped when I saw the therapist, an elongated shadow hovering over Tracy's little blond spinet piano. She had lifted the cover and was moving her fingers over the keys, staring at her own fingers, as if, for one second, they could have been Tracy's. I walked to the end of the long room and watched Deborah's face with a wicked satisfaction.

Deborah's eyes widened as she lifted the piano seat. Sheet music.

'She loved music,' Deborah was saying, her fingers playing over the stapled edges of yellowed piano books. 'Selected

Czerny studies,' she read. I looked into the pile of music. It was a pile of music. "Achievement Series of Piano", Deborah read aloud. 'Tracy would play and play, working her fingers over that keyboard like it was her enemy. Ha, ha! Trills, embellishments, grace notes all came under attack! She was brilliant! I'm telling you she was a genius!' Deborah's hands were running along the ivory keys of the piano again. It was no time to hear about Tracy's musical interludes, it was time to check out the rest of her apartment.

The bedroom. I walked down the little hallway and slipped inside. Tracy had chosen an almost masculine Glen plaid for her coverlets and sheets. A lamp hooded in dark-green glass sat next to a bed, a very big, firm bed. Rubenesque females played with gauze in a framed print on the wall. Inspiration for Tracy?

An exercise bicycle claimed the most important spot by the window. I checked the program. The bicycle was set at its most challenging. I looked at the pedals, remembering Tracy's muscular legs.

It was a good thing Deborah was still busy with the piano, I thought. Who knows what she might do in the bedroom. I shuddered, listening to a few tentative notes being played upon the spinet.

I examined the bedside tables. Reading material: *The Care and Preservation of Manuscripts, The Copyright Reform Act*. Very dry, like old leaves of paper. Like the hands of a dead woman.

There was no soft porn. No drugs. No strap-on under the mattress. Not a sleeping pill or even an aspirin. Only twenty gallons of ice cream in the freezer. I heard a few more sad notes from the spinet in the living room.

Where was Tracy's desk? She must have had an office somewhere. But where? There were no other hallways, no extra bedroom, just a bathroom. Maybe Tracy was short-changed on the second bedroom in her floor plan. Maybe she gave it up for grasspaper silk wallcoverings. Who

154

knows? Who cared? It just meant that there must be a drawer or bureau where Tracy kept all her little notes and bills, somewhere I hadn't seen.

I peered into the closet. Also a neat freak, Tracy employed the double-clipped hangers for the rows of her power suits, just like Frances did. I heard a few more tentative, sad notes from the spinet in the living room as I rifled the drawers and learned more than I ever wanted to know about how Tracy rolled her socks and folded her panties. Where would it be? The clue to Tracy's secret love. My fingers searched among sweaters and sweatsocks. Tracy played tennis. I started on the second dresser. The large drawer at the top yielded the fruit I was looking for. A drawer with a checkbook and a carefully fanned-out row of bills to be paid; a plaid folder trimmed in leather with pockets inside for envelopes, stationery, memorabilia; scraps of papers, the memos and letters and ephemera that every life collected. I unfolded and read every receipt, program and shopping list. There were theatre tickets for the opening of a play at the Rhino next week. Benefit tickets stamped, 'complimentary'. Slipping out of my fingers, the colored papers fluttered through the air on to the carpet.

Bending over I saw another piece of paper on the floor. Had it fallen out with the tickets? Or had it been here all along? A tiny, four-squared piece of paper. I opened it up. Little letters, familiar lettering.

'*I am completely bloodied,*' it began. I shuddered. Bloodied. My God. Was it something she had never sent, or maybe a first draft of the final missal that boomeranged, poisoning the librarian to death. The first notes of a song came from the spinet in the living room. Tracy's handwriting? I remembered Deborah's scrawl from the honesty exercises. This was not it.

' – *I will be taking your life with me.*'

And the rest was gone. Torn off. This was serious business. Somebody had gotten to Tracy before she made good her threat. And it wasn't Helen Thomas. I put the letter in my pocket as I heard a few bars on the spinet come to an end.

'Emma?' A worried tone. Deborah had come out of her mourning reverie. Maybe the whiskey had worn off.

'Yes? I'm almost done – ' I tried to sound reassuring, but my fingers ached to continue their search.

'What are you doing?' Suspicious.

Don't get all noble on me now, Deborah. 'Just looking in the bathroom.' The bedroom, I figured, was not a good word to mention at this point. And I would quickly be on to the bathroom. A place that sometimes yielded more clues than anyone would expect.

I could hear something in Deborah's voice that made me think she needed a little supervision. I would have to be fast. I started quickly through the medicine cabinet. Nary a pill or a powder. Natural cosmetics and some mud packs. Tracy used menstrual pads, not tampons.

There was the usual standard twentieth-century plumbing. Nothing hidden in the toilet tank. The shower and the sink ran hot and cold, just like Tracy. I took my penknife and poked around in the drain. Black curly pubic hair. Could be anybody's. And I didn't have a lab.

Somebody, maybe the police, or maybe the fastidious librarian herself, had emptied the wastecan. There was something sticking to the side, one of those long flat pulls from a sanitary napkin. But then I looked more closely. The pull wasn't right for a sanitary napkin. It was something else, made of some soft absorbent material, the end a pastel blue. I remembered what Deborah had said about Tracy.

'Tracy had a very unhappy upbringing. She had issues. Intimacy issues. Abuse issues. I believe Tracy was severely traumatized as a child. Making love with Tracy Port was the most intense experience of my life . . . She wanted to spill all that love and passion on somebody who didn't care. When you start to care, she cools off . . . She moved on . . . someone . . . fundamentally unavailable . . . It's a common pattern. Not just for lesbians. For the whole of society.'

156

'Emma? What are you doing in here?' It was Deborah. She was taking up most of the doorway of the bathroom. Then she wobbled past me and looked around the bathroom, opening up the medicine chest. She looked accusingly into my face, 'What did you find in here?'

The whiskey *had* worn off. Deborah's eyes didn't hold any more promises. Something shaky, and endlessly freaky was going on in there. I would remember that look in her eyes and the one that followed it for the rest of my life.

Deborah looked behind my back where something loomed. Something familiar and terrifying at the same time. But I didn't have time to look around and see what or who was there. There was a huge explosion.

My ears screamed as my mind struggled to believe my eyes. The entire midsection of Deborah Dunton had turned into a red mist as the cartridge from a twenty-eight-gauge shotgun ripped open her heart.

Chapter Sixteen

The Key to Renquist Falkenberg

*You live in New York. You wait for the delivery.
The men in white coats are coming, carrying the eggs. You
are not ready for this. I feel completely bloodied. Condoms
kept in wallets develop holes.*

*The men push harder, the wheels have turned into squares
and the streets are made of cobblestones. You are in New
York. You have always been in New York.*

*The eggs begin to undulate, yolks softening the shells.
Lumps crawl slowly over the surface, like cats trapped under
the bedclothes. You have eaten off the tops of your fingers. It
doesn't matter.*

*You live in New York. There are clocks on the wall. The
time that they tell is never the present. But there is something
else.*

*They will be fumigating your apartment. You live in New
York. It's a good idea. The apartments have been built by
cockroaches. Rats in the walls recording everything you say.
Outside the whining of sirens bounces off the towers, the
sounds stretch into infinity. There's a noise. It's Deborah
Dunton.*

*The hands of Deborah Dunton are dark. Her white
fingernails are trying to keep her chest together, her heart
inside. Her ribs are a broken cage. Inside, a brown bird is
singing, 'You always hurt the one you love' and I feel completely bloodied.*

Renquist Falkenberg was in front of me. He made little whimpering noises, like a wounded animal. He was bending over something that might have been Deborah Dunton once, but was now a pool of blood in the middle of some arms and legs. Irregular shapes, candy coated in a red slickness floated around white spears. Deborah Dunton's organs, her liver, spleen, intestines, gathered about the ragged white spears that must have been the ends of bones. Deborah's chest had been split open like a baked potato and Renquist Falkenberg had his hands all over her, trying to hold what used to be Deborah Dunton together with his hands. The sounds he made were not human, there was a whimpering and strangling in his throat.

I would have got up and helped him. I would have done a lot of things if I wasn't puking. Puking on a twenty-eight gauge shotgun. I did the cowardly thing. I spat the puke out of my mouth and lay down on the floor and stared at the ceiling. Tracy's pale, seafoam-green ceiling only had a few drops of blood splattered on to it. I listened to Renquist.

'Hang on, Deborah,' he was saying.

'Renquist?'

'Yes?' Just like we'd met in a café. But Renquist was hunched over Deborah Dunton who no longer had a torso. I staggered to my feet. It was too late to save Deborah Dunton but Renquist Falkenberg could do with some help.

I felt in my pocket. The little square of the note was gone. *I feel completely bloodied.*

'C'mon, there's nothing we can do.' I was standing now, somehow, on automatic pilot, not looking at anything except Renquist's face, which had a strange, a very strange expression on it. 'C'mon Renquist.' I had a hand under his huge armpit. I was hoisting him to his feet when his throat started to gurgle.

'Renquist,' I said sternly. 'Just don't look. Don't look. C'mon, we're going to call the cops. Let's go over here. To this corner of the room.' The corner with no blood in it.

Renquist stared at me wide-eyed as if he didn't understand English. It didn't matter. I was just making sounds to fill the air while I got us away from the bloody bag that had been Deborah Dunton.

There were numbers to call for the police. Numbers like 911. I was going to call now. That's just what I was going to do. I was going to call the police.

Then a thought struck me.

I ran out into the hallway and past several doors until I came to Deborah's apartment. The door was open. I remembered Deborah pulling it closed. I remembered the click of the latch.

I walked into the little hallway, through the office of toys and teddy bears into her chintzy living quarters. Someone had trashed Deborah's place. Her stereo was gone. And there were Daddy's big guns hanging on the wall. All except one. Someone had just pried that little padlock off the plexi and helped themselves.

Back in Deborah's office I checked the desk. The key was still hanging above it, on the wall.

I opened the drawer. Frances' *Lesbo-Parthenogenesis* notebook was still inside. I closed the drawer, locked it, returned the key and walked back down the hallway, all twenty-seven steps, into Tracy Port's condo.

Renquist was in the living room looking at the couch as if it might start its engine and race away from him. The blood on his hands was dry. Deborah Dunton was still in the bathroom. I picked up the receiver and called 911 for the second time that day. 'Hello, I would like to report a murder.' As I said it I became aware of a persistent tapping on my shoulder. I put my hand up automatically.

A sticky red hole that used to be my shoulder let me know that this was going to be a fun telephone conversation to get through. I held on to my stomach for the third time and readied my chords for cogent verbal communication.

'Yes, a murder,' I was saying. Renquist Falkenberg was crying, I would have cried too, except that I had a shoulder

160

to try and hold on to and an address to repeat. A long time later, I hung up the phone.

Renquist and I would sit on the sofa, I decided.

The cops would be here in a few minutes. I didn't hear the sirens yet. They would send an ambulance. They always sent an ambulance. *I feel completely bloodied.* What was it about that note? That handwriting?

First I had to hold on to my shoulder. Second, stop Renquist crying before the cops came. He *was* a city supervisor after all. *Our* City Supervisor. I didn't want him to lose it. *I feel completely bloodied.*

I stumbled towards the kitchen. Nope, that's the silver-ware drawer. Then I found the towels. Glen plaid dish towels, neatly folded into squares. I dampened one, two, three, four towels and took them into the living room. I knelt before Renquist and started to wipe his hands with the towels.

I had to think. I had a client to protect. I wouldn't want to spill anything that wasn't in Helen's interests. But you don't fuck around with the cops and murder. They are in the business of gutting your thoughts and by the time they get to be homicide inspectors they can be damn good at it.

'Emma, what are you doing here?' Renquist Falkenberg was suddenly all business. He spoke as if we'd come across each other in a strange country, shopping for vegetables at the same market. A big fog was lifting from his brain.

'Condolence call.' I muttered. 'What were you doing here, Renquist?'

'The memorial meeting, remember?'

'Oh yeah.' Funeral plans I hadn't wanted to be a part of. 'Who else knew you were going to be here?'

'Just you. And Deborah.'

We sat there in the silence and tried to make sense of it all. Had someone been stalking the Supervisor?

I looked into those tiny, red-rimmed orbs that were Renquist Falkenberg's eyes. He had the look of blind ambition. Or maybe that was my own prejudice against politicians. After all, who knows what my eyes looked like at that moment? Then the cops made the scene.

They came inside like they always do, guns drawn, blue barrels flashing like the fingers of the devil. Their eyes and the guns looked around for trouble.

'In the hallway,' I said, hating to spoil their fun but wanting to get the show on the road. They would find the weapon, the body. And then they would try and find out what happened.

They found what was passing for Deborah Dunton and then it was macho time. Another tree-pissing contest began. I could hear them making jokes about ordering pizza, an opportunity to show off their manhood via their iron stomachs.

Next, the Chief Homicide Inspector appeared at the door. I looked him up and down. A gray cashmere suit and the faint smell of cigars. He would be like a thousand other homicide inspectors all across America. With a wife who picked out his clothes for him, a wife who had ambitions to a higher social strata, a wife he would have to get away from at least fourteen hours a day. They would have sex twice a year, once on Christmas and once on the Fourth of July if no one was visiting.

And he would stick the knife in so cleanly I wouldn't know it was there until he twisted it. Oh, I knew this guy. He was like a hundred thousand other Homicide Inspectors in the United States of Violence and cheap weapons.

Just then a cop signaled from the bathroom and the Inspector trudged across the floor. He joined the knot of blue uniforms crowding the hallway, looking at the mess in the bathroom. His mustache twitched like he was smelling a bouquet of roses. From the benignly curious look on his face, he could have been looking at a portrait of his mother.

'Photo detail will be here any minute,' he growled. 'Just stay back, okay?' He bent over and slid a pencil into the trigger ring of the shotgun and pulled it towards him. Then he pushed it back. 'Let's wait,' he said.

He turned and came back across the room towards us. I wondered if he was the type to recognize a City Supervisor.

'Supervisor Falkenberg,' he said with a practiced political sheen. 'Homicide Inspector, Edward C Korian.'

Renquist shook his hand. Renquist, in fact, shook all over. His hands trembled and his eyes looked almost pleading. 'Please, sit down, sir,' Korian said, comforting the witness, another traumatized victim of crime. Then he looked over at me.

I wasn't going to get the pillow treatment, I could tell.

'So, which one of you called?'

'I did.'

'Okay. Who are you? Let's start there.'

'My name is Emma Victor.'

'Emma Victor, oh yes.' His blue eyes narrowed. It wasn't a good sign. Name recognition with cops is not what I aspire to. Inspector Korian held his hand out in what might have passed for chivalry and put it under my elbow.

'I won't break, you know,' I pulled my arm away.

'Sure, Miss Victor.' He waved me over to the breakfast nook with a quick, 'Excuse me, Supervisor.' But Renquist was on his cellular phone now, talking to Allen Boone.

Korian pulled out a chair for me from the high-gloss formica table. I sat down carefully and took my hand away from my shoulder. I decided not to look at whatever might have been on my hand. I kept my face still. It was a real meditation. I just put that shoulder way into outer space. Inspector Korian's eyes held something that might, just might, have passed for respect.

'Okay, Miss Victor. Now, let's get back to the story.'

Miss Victor. It bode worse.

'I was in the bathroom and Deborah – '

'That's – ?' his head flicked towards the hallway.

'Yes. She came into the bathroom and walked past me to the medicine chest. I turned round to watch her. Then I saw her being shot. She was shot from behind me. The next I knew there was a shotgun at my feet and Renquist had appeared.'

I was getting a headache from trying to keep my face still. The front of my skin seemed to stiffen and harden.

'And then what happened?'

'I lay down, puked a few times on the gun, stood up again, drew Renquist away from Deborah's body and sat him on the couch. I called 911 and then I wiped off his hands.'

'That's all?'

'That's all.'

'Hmm!' The Inspector seemed amused. He looked around the apartment, at Tracy's neutered interior, the blood spatters on the wall, the wallpaper, the back of some sidechairs. His eyes saw everything: the bay view, the books, the blond spinet piano. Then his eyes returned to mine.

'So this Deborah. She lived here?'

'She lived down the hall.'

The Inspector smiled. 'You know whose apartment this is, Miss Victor?'

I nodded.

'I suggest you start from the beginning. And don't leave anything out. I like the details. Details make me happy.'

I told him I had been at the Howard Blooming Lesbian and Gay Memorial Archive Gala Dinner – the one where the murder had taken place. Korian didn't twitch a muscle or flick a lash, but I knew being a lesbian wouldn't exactly endear me to him. I told him that I remembered that a photographer by the name of Gurl Jesus had taken photos of our dinner table. I had gone to Gurl Jesus' apartment this morning and found her dead. I called 911 at 10.23 and reported the homicide.

Inspector Korian's face was carefully composed granite now. 'This is your second homicide call in a day, Miss Victor?'

'Yes.'

164

'You've witnessed three murders in a weekend?'

I didn't say anything.

'So, you left this Gurl Jesus' apartment about 10.15. Why did you go there precisely, Miss Victor?

'I was hoping to find some negatives of the photos.'

'And?'

'Gurl Jesus used a Polaroid.'

'And then you came here?'

'I went home first. Then Renquist called me to say that there was a meeting at Deborah's to organize a funeral – a public memorial – for Tracy Port. That gave me an idea. I thought I would drift by and ask Deborah a few questions first. I knew that she had had a romantic involvement with Tracy, one that didn't turn out in her favor.

'I thought I would ask Deborah if she remembered anything suspicious. We talked and she agreed to show me Tracy's apartment.'

'Just like that.' Korian did something with his lips that might have been called a smile. But it wasn't nice.

'I think she wanted to see the place. She was drunk; she had AB Alcohol Breath.'

'Take me back to Gurl Jesus, Miss Victor. You came across a murder scene, walked around it for a while, and then you were kind enough to let us know about it.'

'I wouldn't call it kindness.'

'I wouldn't call it smart, Miss Victor.'

'I don't have anything to hide. I'm investigating on behalf of a client.'

'Oh, a *client*!' Inspector Korian leaned back and nodded his head slowly.

'I work for Willie Rossini – the lawyer? She's defending Helen Thomas against the charge of murdering Tracy Port.'

'Really! Isn't that interesting? Tell me more about it.'

'I picked up Helen this morning from jail.'

Korian sighed, 'Listen Miss Victor, this isn't a detective novel. And you're not Mickey Spillane.'

'Did I ever *want* to be Mickey Spillane, Inspector Korian? I don't get your point.'

'My point, Miss Victor, is that you are tripping over too many dead bodies to make anybody comfortable with the idea of letting you wander around loose.' He jerked his head at someone behind my back. I looked around and saw a paramedic standing behind me. Korian waved his hand and I knew what was going to happen.

A guy from photo detail licked his lips as the paramedic carefully clipped away what was left of my shirt sleeve. There was a long black gouge out of one side of my shoulder with burnt threads of white T-shirt sticking out, hard with dried blood.

Men murmured in the background. There were no women at this crime scene. My female arm felt exposed in this world of men and blood.

Snip, snip, snip. I could almost see inside now. Something had been burnt. It reminded me very strongly of hot dogs on a grill and I realized it was my upper arm.

When the wound was fully revealed I felt the flash of a camera bulb as someone took a mug shot of my shoulder.

'Let me tell you something, Miss Victor. You keep your smart ass out of this case. You hear me? I don't want to hear about you at any crime scenes or asking questions of anyone involved in this case, you understand me? Or I will get a court order to cool your heels in jail with the kind of company that would just love to bust that lovely poker face of yours.'

'Now, Supervisor Renquist,' the Inspector turned away from me as easily as a knife through warm butter. 'I think we need to talk about diplomatic protection – ' Korian was already over with Falkenberg, a palsy arm around the huge City Supervisor. Then a cop emerged from the bathroom with a slick triangle of paper, dripping red off the edge of his tweezers. A little cellophane bag, ready to receive the piece of evidence hung loosely beneath it. A little blood had dripped into the bag, and was making a red line at the bottom of the plastic.

'Look what I found!' the cop muttered, happy as a kid with his first trout.

He turned his head at an impossible angle and read words that were apparently inscribed there. '*I feel –* '

'I would like to put you in touch with Dignitary Duty, Supervisor, if only for the next few days,' Korian was telling Renquist. 'We have a suite at the St Francis Hotel. There's a special entrance and elevator. We think it would be a good idea.'

Inspector Korian walked Renquist away, and I felt the paramedic slapping a bandage on my wound. My naked shoulder, my beautiful naked shoulder had a bite out of it and Frances, the woman I loved, was nowhere within reach.

From the bathroom, the cops were cracking jokes.

'You know what they call the gay cemetery? Har, har, har.'

'No?'

'Out and *over*.'

Ha! Ha! Ha!

Detective Korian looked over at me. 'I guess I'll be seeing you later,' he said. I managed to look totally blank.

I continued to hold my face rigid and keep myself moving until I got out of the building.

Then I sat down on the curb and tried to let my face relax. When I finally succeeded, for a moment, just a moment, my whole view of the Bay Bridge was awash with tears.

Chapter Seventeen

Blind Date

Someone followed me to the Castro, someone with squealing brakes. I took a circuitous route. The individual followed.

The likelihood of the same car taking the same route from the Mission to the Castro was too small to make this coincidence. Or to make him that careless. This was not exactly a tail. This was someone who wanted to make contact. Someone with a mustache, and a late model Ford.

I plunged into the intersection of Eighteenth and Castro Street, the busy valley full of buses, cars and pedestrians. I pulled into a truck-loading zone in front of the twenty-four hour Walgreens. My new-found friend got a space in the parking lot just beyond.

Walgreens was busy. I went to the back and picked up some packages of sterile gauze and first aid tape that supposedly *breathed*. Then I checked out the section with condoms, gels, diaphragms and spermicides and made my choice, leaving the drugstore with the goods in a small plastic bag.

I drove down Market, my friend a cool stoplight behind me. Pulling into a red zone just outside Café Flor, I put an old parking ticket under my windshield. Let the mustache-man find a legal parking space. If he had to. I would take my chances on a red square. Three-fifteen. I hoped it would give me time, time to make a few phone calls.

I ducked behind the wood dividers that fenced the patio

section of the café from the street. The outdoor phone booth was free. I dialed my own number and scanned the patio crowd. The patio crowd, some of them, scanned me. I punched in my answer code and heard the rewinding voice of Rose Baynetta.

'*Emma, for your information, Eleanor DeWade, the name on Fresca's license plate, was a "DB".*'

'DB'. A dead baby.

'*Born 1967, Died 1968,*' Rose continued, '*Youngstown, Ohio.*'

So, Fresca Alcazon had constructed an identity for herself out of the death of an infant twenty-five years ago. '*See you later, Emma. Let's try for a quiet evening.*'

But it wasn't likely. I thought I saw mustache ducking behind a corner at the front of the patio, where small one-person tables were shielded from my view. Popping in the backdoor I found the restroom free. The rest was easy.

I opened the Walgreens bag, found the box inside and read the instructions carefully. I tore the box open. Sliding the silk boxers off my waist and letting them drift to my knees I completed the task. The result was as expected. I gave my shoulder a quick check before I left the restroom. I would live.

Returning to the bar I stood in line for a double cappuccino. I hadn't had a meal for sixteen hours. But I was far too wired to think about food. Eying the backs of heads outside the front window I watched a line of people hunched over tables, staring into their coffees. I would stay inside, I thought, picking up my drink and warming my hands as I walked over to a tiled table.

An offering of old and new magazines lay in the corner. I picked up an old *OUT* magazine, one with k d lang on the cover. I held her up in front of me, like some kind of talisman, some kind of protection. I waited. I looked at the pictures. I saw nothing. Time passed reluctantly.

Out of the smoke and conversation someone emerged and sat down next to me. *He* carried a *New York Times*, and wore a blue work shirt, khaki pants. When I felt comfortable enough to lower my magazine, I found a wary-looking person who needed a shave. He didn't like me either.

'Nine-four-one, thirteen-forty-seven.' He barely moved his lips.

It took a moment to sink in. 941–1347.

I nodded.

'In ten minutes. Now point outside to that window.'

I pointed outside, across Market Street to the Baghdad Café. Mustache thanked me, finished his espresso in a gulp, and was gone.

I stared at some glossy fashion pages. Time passed even more reluctantly. Ten minutes later I returned to the phone booth and called the number.

'Hello?'

'Hi. This is Emma Victor.'

'Emma, old gal, hey, what's doin' man? Georgette told me ah should look you up when I pass into town.'

'Georgette, yeah? How's she doing?'

'Fine. You going to be home about five o'clock? I want to stop by, say hello.'

'Sure. It will be nice to see you.'

I called Rose again and left her a message. *'I've got a date. Five o clock. Hope you can make it.'*

First I wanted to see Carla Ribera. It was the kind of thing that would get me in trouble with Inspector Ed Korian, but what the hell.

The fog had engulfed Glen Park, where Carla had turned a storefront into a photography studio. I hadn't called earlier. I wanted to be a surprise. I wasn't.

Carla's dress had been recently pressed and her lipstick was fresh. She licked her lips as she saw me at the door.

'Emma! How unexpected! Come in!'

'I've always wanted to see your place, Carla!' I went inside to the tune of Carla's phone ringing.

'Oh, excuse me.' Carla's charm bracelet jangled as she

threw a few jet black curls over her shoulder, turned and raced down a hallway. 'Have a seat, I'll be right back.'

Carla's huge sofa, shaped like two big red lips in the middle of her showroom, was the only available seating. I settled myself into it. It was like a kiss, a kiss that would eat me. I stared at the walls that featured Carla's work.

Photographs, mounted on board, were suspended along a curving wall. The figures of women printed on metallic paper seemed to float in the middle of the room.

Runway models anyone? Carla had had them all in front of her lens. Seductive waifs. Voluptuous sluts. Fashion skeletons with barbed hips. Rounded young girls fresh from the shower.

'Can I offer you something, Emma?' Carla was striding back into the room. She looked at me, her arms folded. 'Beer, wine cooler?'

'Soda pop. Any kind.'

Ribera turned her attention to a section of the wall. As she tapped on an almost hidden seam, a door slid noiselessly open, revealing rows of liquor bottles. A small refrigerator, lined with rows of glasses, was held in place by rounded brass rails.

Carla didn't stand, she planted herself, like a two hundred year old tree, feet spread wide apart as she poured herself a Scotch. I remembered how much Rose had been in love with Carla. There was a way the woman pulled the tab off my soda with a casual flick of the wrist and a certain tenderness as she listened to the bubbles flow over the ice. Tenderness or calculation. Carla had chosen a cut-throat business.

Carla brought me the soda with a twist of lemon. She jiggled the glass for a moment before she turned around.

'How's Frances?' Carla asked.

'Fine. Carla, can I ask you a question?'

'Sure.'

'I want to ask you about the baptism at the Universal Church.'

The room was suddenly so silent the bubbles in my drink sounded like a geyser.

'I don't know what you're talking about.'

'The scrapbook that Berniece said you stole.'

'Berniece is getting Alzheimer's,' Carla said. 'Pretty soon she'll forget to light her oven when she turns it on.'

'I hope that's not as nasty as it sounds, Carla. Deborah Dunton was murdered today.'

I watched Carla's face. It moved and twisted. Nervous fingers stretched out and plucked the last Gauloise out of a cellophane packet. She curled the outer cellophane wrapper into a ball in her fist and tossed it into the garbage can. She turned around towards me, balanced one leg over another, twitched her foot a few times impatiently, lit her cigarette, shook the match out and asked me what my business was.

'Rose told me that you took the photographs at the Universal Church baptism.'

'Rose talks a lot.'

'Yeah. Sort of endearing, really.'

'Endearing?' Carla snorted. 'My God, that woman is her own worst enemy.'

'The scrapbook, Carla, do you have it?'

'No.'

'I'd like to look at it.'

'I said I don't have it, Victor.' Carla smiled. 'With a little lighting, Emma, I could make you every dyke's dream.'

'Without any lighting I've been a few dykes' nightmare. Listen, Carla, are you going to show me the scrapbook?'

'I really don't have it, Emma. I don't.'

'Okay. How long have you known Larry Boznian?'

'Larry?' Pause. Sucking on her Gauloise. One, two quick drags. 'Eight, maybe ten years.' She looked down, tamping her cigarette in the ashtray. I met him at a furniture exhibit in Barcelona. He was showing chairs that year.'

'Do you know anything about where he's from? Originally?'

'No. Emma, you really should let me take your photo sometime.'

'Sure, Carla, sure.'

'Well, I hate to kick you out –'

'Okay,' I finished my soda and let myself be brushed off. Carla showed me to her stainless steel door and locked it after it closed. I walked to my car, started it and drove around the block.

It was garbage night in Glen Park. The bottle collectors would be coming as soon as it was dark. Charles Dickens' California.

I opened the car door quietly, slipped outside, and crouched behind the skirt of eucalyptuses across the street from Carla's studio. From between the fringe of curling leaves I saw lights going on in her room. Snap! Snap! Then Carla came out the back door and deposited a big bag of garbage. I could see her silhouette as she raised the lid of the can. Then there was a heavy bang and the rattle of the lid being shut.

Carla paused for a moment, peering out through the fog. She locked her door, got into her white Mazzerati and drove away. I watched the car purr off into the distance.

Carla's garbage can was a gift indeed. Inside a big black opaque bag was a nice collection of Newcastle Bitter bottles. And underneath those, and some long ribbons of exposed negatives, was Berniece Able's scrapbook.

I couldn't make it back to the car quickly enough. I drove down the block, until I found a deserted spot. Hands shaking, I leafed quickly through the scrapbook. There it was. The Universal Church baptism. The event which had sent Jeb Flynne over the edge.

I remembered that day. It had been warm and sunny, a Sunday morning with a gospel chorus. Renquist Falkenberg had been glad-handing the crowd while Howard stood, almost shyly. And Allen was there too. The first hate notes had arrived that very morning.

I peered closer at the photo. At the people stepping up to have their infants baptized. There was one white woman with a baby. She looked familiar. One of the first lesbian mothers perhaps? And then I looked closer at her child. The infant was beautiful. A brown baby girl with a small gale force of a squall coming out of her mouth. People were actually clapping their hands on their ears! The baby's mouth became wider and wider as I moved in closer. And then I saw it. There was no mistaking the birthmark on that tiny neck, a deep, rich, ruby-red stain.

Then I remembered the handwriting on the note and why it was so familiar.

And now I knew why Carla had stolen Berniece Able's scrapbook. And I knew why I wasn't going to give it back. I put a finger underneath the photograph of the baptism and tugged at it. The gummed cellophane, which Allen found so objectionable, loosened and the scrapbook gave up one of its memories. I folded the photo into a piece of index paper, tucked it inside my jacket, and headed home. After all, I had a date.

He showed up at a decent seven minutes past five. Seven minutes for me to sweat through my deodorant and wonder if I could take up smoking and still live in California. I opened the door. The individual who stood there was around five foot eleven, a middleweight. He would be strong. 'Ralph Chesterton,' this charmer said formally, and held out his hand.

I grabbed his forearm and pulled as hard as I could. Rose wheeled up right behind him and had Fresca's little .22 aimed somewhere below his neck. She then backed slowly away. It wasn't easy in a wheelchair, but Rose did just fine.

'Don't move,' I barked. 'The woman behind you is familiar with firearms. The revolver is cocked and there is a shell in the chamber. It's a .22. Doesn't do a lot of damage, but she wouldn't mind putting you in a wheelchair. I believe she's aiming for your spine.'

'Okay, okay, but – '

'Shut up.' There is nothing in the world like having a gun trained on someone. Every little move could be a checkmate that gets somebody killed.

I patted the man down, emptying his pockets. It wasn't fun. I turned up an ankle holster with a Smith and Wesson in it on the first round. After I'd relieved him of that I found his money clip, a thousand dollars in notes, and some change.

'Hey, look – ' he started again.

'Shut *up*,' I yelled and jerked my head for Rose to wheel closer. 'Listen buddy,' I pushed him into a chair. 'I'm really angry with you, you understand?' I had his hair in my hand. It felt terrible, but there was a hate inside of me that made me not want to let go. This was the character that had trashed my house. I was sure of it.

I reached behind me for the duct tape and pushed his hands behind the chair, I worked quickly, trying to keep an eye on this joker, on his feet, head; on Rose; on the windows and doors. Only when I had his hands taped behind his back, his chest and feet firmly bound, could I take a breath. Looking him over, a big beefy character I could have never taken, I felt myself getting angrier.

'Emma,' Rose cautioned.

'What's your story, dickhead?'

'Listen – ' His face was red.

'Why should I listen to you, creep? Why shouldn't I just let Rose give it to you. An intruder against a woman in a wheelchair.'

'I'll tell you why you'll listen, Victor. There are a lot of reasons. And some of them have to do with why you made the date with me in the first place. I'm interested in someone you've just gotten to know. And if you can give me a lead on that person there is a thousand dollars in it for you.'

'Why shouldn't I just take it?'

'Because, Miss Victor, you want to know who I am. Don't you?'

'Yeah, shithead, I really want to know. Who the fuck are you?'

'I'll give you a number and you dial it. If you hold the phone by my head I'll say something into it, okay? They'll get a voiceprint identification. They'll clear me, okay?'

'Shall I give him the phone, Rose?'

'Sure. Why not. Give him the phone.' Rose's voice was a monotone. The man recited some numbers. I dialed the unfamiliar area code and the following seven digits according to his instructions. I held the phone to his face.

'Okay, Chesterton for clearance,' he said clearly into the receiver. 'Give them a description.'

'*Hold.*' I took the receiver back. It was an automatic voice. A few seconds later, it parroted a portrait of the man sitting in front of me. '*Twenty-nine, five foot ten, one hundred and seventy-five pounds, blue eyes, pale complexion, large mole under right armpit, scar on both large toes at base of nails. Chesterton is on duty with the Treasury Department.*'

'Let's *not* take off his shoes,' Rose said.

'Treasury department,' I looked the guy up and down. It was really going to be hard to *un*tape him. 'Really?' I tried to look impressed.

'Yep,' he said confidently.

'You know, it's really not polite to go calling on ladies with guns.'

'You're no lady.'

'Careful, Emma,' Rose cautioned quietly from her chair.

'You two intend to untie me now?' he smirked.

'Sure.'

I cut the tape and started to tear it off of his clothes. When enough of it was loose he stood up and pulled off the rest with a pinched expression. I invited him to sit down on the couch. I offered him a Scotch. I even gave him back his gun.

'Okay.' He took the gun first, then the drink. 'Miss Victor, we believe that you know someone who is involved in a sophisticated money laundering operation. We have reason to believe that you know this person.' He showed me a xeroxed photo. It was Fresca Alcazon.

'Ramona Hurst,' he said. 'Sound familiar?'

Footsteps on the roof. The house professionally tossed. Christ, he'd even taken the wall sockets off! What the hell had he expected to find in there?

I shrugged my shoulders. 'Come on, Miss Victor. We saw you with her. We followed you here to your residence where you kept her busy for three hours.'

'She looks like someone I met the other night.' I admitted, grudgingly.

'What was her name?'

'Fresca.'

'That's it?'

'Yeah.'

'Well, she was driving a BMW motorcycle which was bought with cash in Switzerland, from a less-than-reputable dealer. The cash she used came from a bank robbery twenty-five years ago. A bank robbery where four people were killed. A thousand dollars for a pointer, Miss Victor. Just tell us if you have another date with this individual. A phone number, perhaps?'

'Hell would freeze over before I gave you any number, bub. Get a subpœna. Get a warrant. But most of all, get the fuck out of my house.' I pushed him into the doorway.

'Miss Victor, these people are armed and dangerous – . That's why there's been all this sneak and creep stuff. We don't want them to know we're on to them. And we don't want to endanger you. We have to stop them, Miss Victor.'

'*You're* armed and dangerous. Who's stopping you?'

I slammed the door, missing his fingertips by a nano-second. Rose and I sat there in the silence. 'I hope your tax returns look good, Miss Victor,' he yelled into the wood. Chesterton thundered down the stairs.

'Tsk, tsk, tsk,' said Rose. 'Congress just isn't doing its job, Emma.' The phone was ringing.

It was Fresca Alcazon. Or Ramona Hurst. Or Eleanor DeWade. It was of the greatest urgency that she meet me at the Archive. And that I take public transportation to get there.

Chapter Eighteen

Vaulting Fresca

I took the Mission Street bus. It started and stopped. People got off and on. And some people got on when I did and stayed.

He was a bit overweight, but I wouldn't let his stocky build fool me. He would be fit, strong. And possibly armed.

I got off the Mission Street bus at 18th. I was in luck. The 18th Street bus was waiting for me. It set off right away, but it was a slow bus route. I sat in the back and watched my tail catch up with us at every stop.

He was six feet tall, with a buzz cut, a baggy gray hooded sweatshirt, a backpack and a baseball hat screwed on backwards. He had Converse sneakers and the loping walk of a teenager. He was the image of thousands of other teenagers. But this one was meant for me.

He faded from view around Dolores Park. The bus continued through the Castro and went up the steep hill on the other side of Market. When it reached the top it stopped. I got off and looked around me. I started down the lane that would lead me to the Archive. It loomed large and gray and evil, like a Transylvanian castle.

Then I heard him. The snapping of a twig. Someone rustling through the pine needle carpet. I felt the branches scratching my cheeks. I didn't care. When the baseball cap fell off I felt no sadness. When she held me in her arms, tightly, expectantly, I didn't feel the fog or any impending sense of doom. My hands ran over the corded muscles that rode along the top of her leg. I looked into the caraway seed eyes, at the expectant smile that was stretching large across her face. Her face seemed big and bare as the moon, now that she had no hair.

Fresca Alcazon had shaved her head. Had transformed herself into a boy. Her hug revealed extra padding in her shirt, hiding her breasts, but her breasts were there. We did a slow dance, feverish with reunion, the moon and the danger. She pulled me closer still.

'Emma. God, I'm so glad to see you. I brought you something.'

'Fresca. I brought you something too.' There was no way to break it gently.

'What?' She had caught the warning tone in my voice.

'A photograph.' I watched her face take care of itself. 'A photograph of your baptism.' The lips pressed together, the eyes fled behind a thousand doors. She turned around and I heard her fill her lungs with fog. Then, slowly, she let the long breath out into the night. When she turned around she was someone new. Someone that wasn't quite Fresca Alcazon any more.

'You know,' she stated flatly. Her backpack fell to the ground.

'Yes.'

A sad grin tugged at her lips. 'So what are you going to do about it?'

'Help you.'

'Yeah, sure!' she chortled wryly, her shoulders riding up. 'Why would you help me. You *know* who I am.'

'The undercover life must be hard.' I checked this fact with her face. There was a history of running and fear there, a life that was unimaginable except to Fresca Alcazon. She had spent her entire life underground.

'Larry makes it difficult.'

'I'll bet. Why did Larry choose such a high profile occupation, Fresca? Why on earth paint that ceiling at the Archive?'

'I know, it was stupid. But I'd met Carla in Rome and she'd tried to convince us that we could move back to the States. The commission for the mural was money we needed. We didn't think the Archive opening would be such a big event. It felt so unlikely that anyone would recognize Larry. And he's such a *good* artist. This was his chance to realize an artistic dream.'

'Larry needs help, Fresca.'

'Yeah,' she sighed, 'I know. He's going to slip into that bottle and drown.'

'You can't save him. Nobody can.'

'But, Emma,' Fresca's voice held a note of desperation. 'I have to save Larry. I can't *desert* him. He's all I've got. He's been my life, our life – '

'I know,' I said gently, quietly. 'Family is important to me, too.'

Fresca put up a fight against tears and lost. I held her in my arms and told her that I knew all about it. I told her that she didn't have to be afraid of me. Now that I knew what the strange relationship of Larry Boznian and Fresca Alcazon was all about.

Larry Boznian, the man who was having such a hard time with the bottle lately, was treading an identity tightrope and not doing such a good job of it. Larry Boznian had had to keep his balance for a long time, ever since he built the bomb that blew up the apartment that Fresca had been in. Being wanted on four counts of murder was no mean history. Being sought after all the time had made life dangerous.

Walls of fear, fear of cages, of running, of fake passports and dual nationalities flickered inside Fresca's eyes.

'Fresca.' I unfolded the piece of index paper. It was white and clean, the precious image nestling inside. I handled it carefully. I wanted to show respect for the moment in history which, if revealed, could ruin lives.

There she was in the photos, with that ruby-red birthmark on her neck. Very recognizable. Less instantly recognizable, but obvious enough when you looked at the photo closely, was the identity of the woman holding Fresca in her arms. Fresca's mother was Laurie Leiss. And Laurie Leiss looked familiar in more ways than one. She was the woman I had seen in the car park. She was also Larry Boznian.

Fresca reached out for the photo.

'Uh-uh, not so fast.' I pulled the photo out of her reach. 'I want some answers. Let's go back. Back to when I gave Laurie the twenty thousand bucks in the parking lot in Sacramento.'

'Yes, that was the final step,' Fresca said. 'We'd been running for seven years. I remember a blur of old farm houses, hideouts. We wanted out of the country. Mom wanted to take the final step. She wanted to go to Sweden and have the operation. She wanted to live and be an artist in Europe. She knew it would be easier as a man. Everything is easier as a *man*, Emma, you wouldn't believe.'

'I would, I would. But I have a question, Fresca. Why did Howard give Laurie the twenty thousand dollars? It wasn't family loyalty, was it?'

Fresca snorted.

'Your mother's group took the explosives for their revolutionary agenda from Howard's labs, did they, Fresca? And Laurie had some proof of this didn't she? Proof she used to blackmail Howard.'

Fresca nodded.

'Then they blew up that brownstone in New York. But it's dangerous taking your baby on a bombing expedition, isn't it Fresca? Bombs can go off before you get out. And that's how you got your quilted leg.'

Pause. 'That's right. I've seen a lot of pretty strange doctors in my day, Emma.'

'I'll bet.' I imagined Fresca as a baby, being taken to medical men who'd mend wounds without questions. No wonder her leg was a bit of a botch job. Then I knew what I was going to do.

'Fresca, soon I'll have the other key to Howard Blooming's safety deposit box in the Archive. I'll give you thirty seconds to look inside to see if there's anything you want. Then you give me back the key. That's what I'm doing and that's all I'm doing.'

'Why would you do that for me, Emma?'

But we both knew the answer to that. 'What do you think you're going to find in that box? What was worth you and Larry mugging me for?'

'We were afraid,' she began slowly. 'We were terrified that Howard had gotten hold of the documents of the sex change operation that Mom had had in Sweden. I don't know how he got them. Or if he really ever had them. But once, when Mom called him he said he knew what her real identity was. And if she didn't keep away from him he would blow her cover wide open.'

I let the historical facts jiggle around in my head. Events assumed new places, people new identities. The past was a different place than I'd thought I'd inhabited.

'Those rumors about Howard's final papers always worried us. Then we heard David Stimpson was going back to San Francisco to sell up and move for good. We were terrified that he'd decide to have the papers published.'

'So you started to follow David – and then you were after me. I locked eyes with Fresca. It was hard not to smile. I was glad that we'd met – one way or the other.

'Okay, Fresca, I'll meet you here the day after tomorrow. The library opens at nine. Meet me here at 8 am. I'll manage to get us in.'

'Honey, you are *hot*,' Fresca said appreciatively.

'No kidding. We're both hot.'

'What do you mean?'

'I've got a Homicide Inspector on my ass. Somebody blew away Deborah Dunton today with a shotgun. Got any ideas?'

Fresca knew just what I meant. 'Larry is – was – a revolutionary. He didn't just *kill* people – '

'No, he killed them for a cause.' I almost smiled, almost,

but not quite. But I didn't think Larry Boznian was Deborah Dunton's killer. I just wanted to check the facts on Fresca's face. Larry Boznian was just a drunk on the lamb.

'And you've got the Treasury Department on your ass, Fresca.'

'What?'

I nodded slowly. 'Someone came over to my house to offer me a thousand dollars for your phone number.'

'Fuck!' Fresca stamped her foot on the ground, hard.

We both stood there and let the implications sink in. Fresca wouldn't be sticking around for long. But she'd always known that. Fresca could never stay in one place for more than a day or two. No wonder she'd needed to see me fast. She'd had to have Howard's box and she didn't have time to waste.

Fresca gave me a sudden hug. 'Hey, Emma, it's really fun to tail you, you know that?' She was nuzzling my neck. 'I have a present for you.' She reached for her backpack. Inside, carefully wrapped in a white linen tea towel was a book, brown, with gold lettering.'

'*The Making of the Americans*,' I read. 'It's lovely, Fresca.'

'Open it up, Emma.' Fresca put the parchment like vellum against my cheek. 'It's cool, almost soft, isn't it?' She displayed the signature, Gertrude Stein, in a bold stroke across the inner board. 'One of Five.'

'It's beautiful,' I turned it over in my hands. Fresca slipped her hand inside my shirt, found my breast, her fingertips against my tightening nipples.

Our shirts both came off, and there was no fog at all. Fresca knelt in front of me. Her breasts were silken and they hung, loose, gifts of soft fruit. She worked her way down my body, fingertips and lips in precious counterpoint. I could feel the Stein volume next to me, the deckled edge of the pages, Fresca's mouth between my thighs, bringing me close.

> *Lifting belly with me.*
> *You inquire. What you do then.*

Pushing.
Thank you so much.
And lend a hand.
What is lifting belly now.
My baby.
Always sincerely.
Lifting belly says it there.
Thank you for the cream.
Lifting belly tenderly.
A remarkable piece of intuition.

Chapter Nineteen

Riot

Sirens interrupted a final embrace. Fresca pulled away from me. I saw colors flashing on her face. Red, black, red, black. A cherry light whizzed down the street alongside of us. Towards the Civic Center.

That's when I heard the familiar sounds. Distant chanting. Loud and fierce. An ocean of rage. People were running down the street. Glass was breaking. A police car zoomed by, summoned to a barrier position perhaps. A central command had already been set up.

'God, Emma, I want you to have me,' Fresca was kissing me hard. 'Fuck me later, baby, baby, later—' She was throwing her clothes on quickly. Then she was running.

'Where are you going?' I shouted after her.

'Where do I ever go? To try and find Mom.' I caught the glimmer of something wet and dark on her cheek. And then she was gone.

There were voices all around me now. Clots of people, planning, laughing, angry. Within seconds my treadless tennies hit the pavement.

I remembered this part. You saw the flames. You ran *towards* them. Towards, of course, the temples of government, those pompous sugar tart castles in the center of town. The dome of City Hall – taller even than the Capitol dome, as the tourist guides proudly pointed out – came into view. From the Civic Center, a flame gushed forth into the night. People were yelling, a flat backdrop of chants. What were they saying? '*Sheebbeeen! Sheebbeeen!*' A rhythm against the running feet. I moved, hypnotized, towards the conflagration.

All around me police cars exploded, their gas tanks popping, their shattered shells forming vicious shrapnel which rained all around us. Gallons of gas added to the fountain of flame which threatened to engulf the entire Civic Center.

It was nearly seven o'clock. I looked behind me. A new generation of twenty-nothing dykes, and an army of young men who had nothing to lose in this economy, were running around in groups that looked almost happy. 'We're here, we're queer. Get used to *it!*'

The crowd seemed to thin out as I got closer to the center. The heat from the flames made the small street an oven. And then I saw the front line. Four separate groups of people, in perfect concert, had picked up a large construction railing. They had stripped the legs from the thirty-foot metal barricade. They held their communal spear, gripping tight, listening to the chants.

The crowd was split now. Some cried 'No violence! No violence!' and someone else yelled 'Fuck you!' A cheer went up as the spear bearers aimed the jousting lance at the very door of the federal building.

The door was covered with a grille featuring the golden goddess of justice and a bald eagle above her head. The goddess was blindfolded, and the bald eagle seemed to look down slyly at her breasts.

As the spear was aimed at the door the crowds roared in approval. Even the 'No violence' faction were silenced by the sight of this mighty beam aimed at the mockery they thought justice to be in America.

More people took hold of the beam. Men and women, black, brown and white, old and young, the most self-selected rainbow group I had ever seen, hugged their lance and started to march forward.

They picked up steam as they ran towards the door and with a deafening roar of metal, 'Justice' was punctured through the stomach. The crowds cheered. More battering rams were hoisted aloft and thirty-foot spears were aimed at the windows. One by one the heavy glass sheets shattered.

'*Shebbeee! Sheeebeee! Shebfee!*'

Other groups marched towards the Federal building, climbed up on the embankment and crawled inside. Chairs, paper, computers and keyboards flew out of the windows and crashed on to the pavements.

I turned on my transistor radio and tuned into the twenty-four hour news channel. I listened to the din around me echoed inside the little plastic box and then I heard the voice of a journalist frantically describing the scene before us.

'*In front of me tonight, one of the worst civil riots in the history of San Francisco, the result of an attempt being made on the life of City Supervisor Renquist Falkenberg. Official sources, who decline to be identified, have confirmed that a threatening note at the scene of a recent murder was written by assassin, Jeb Flynne. Although Flynne was believed to have committed suicide, several murders recently in San Francisco have been linked to the assassin.*'

'*I feel completely bloodied.*' The handwriting had been familiar. But it had not been Tracy's handwriting. It had been Jeb Flynne's.

That's when I realized what the two-word chant had been. Jeb Flynne. Jeb Flynne.

The original battering group was still going at Justice. The 'No violence' chants were weaker. Photographers were arriving at the scene. The popping of breaking windows was counterpointed with flashbulbs, white blasts against the inferno of bursting gas tanks and the black, acrid smoke of cop-car tires.

A fax machine landed at my feet with a crash – cracked plastic, glimmering circuit boards and a lot of little screws. I pulled back behind the corner of a building, out of the line of fire and, just like everyone else, watched the battering group break into the temple of justice.

A flurry of burning papers flew out of the building. I picked up one of the papers as it drifted by on the wind. Through the smoke I could read, 'Workmen's compensation' and an address in Modesto.

There was a bright pink flare and someone screamed. The Tactical Squad had arrived. I watched them moving forward as one, a slow, relentless march of faceless creatures, with helmets. Gas masks covered their features, triads of eyes and mouth making them look more like insects from a low grade B-movie than human beings.

The street stilled, the crowd looked at the squad for one long second. The battering ram was hoisted up higher under the rebels' arms. Sweating brown, white, tan, purple, faces reflected anger and utter determination.

'Sources close to the police force have leaked the news that handwriting on notes received both by the City Supervisor Renquist Falkenberg and by the police has been positively identified as that of assassin, Jeb Flynne. Flynne, who allegedly committed suicide while in a jail in Los Angeles five years ago – Here! Wait a second – here is Supervisor Renquist Falkenberg now! The Supervisor has been busy with aides preparing a statement since rioting broke out which nearly destroyed the Federal Building.'

I was standing at the Civic Center. The tactical squad had done their work. The riot was over, the demonstrators gone.

And then the unmistakable tones of Renquist Falkenberg floated over the airwaves: the deep reasonable, velvet voice, speaking from his suite at the St Francis.

'I would like to ask the lesbian and gay communities, all of the communities of San Francisco, to try to come together in this difficult, difficult, time. There are those who say that Jeb Flynne is alive. If that is true, then he will be brought to Justice. In the meantime we must continue to live our lives with the kind of integrity that will help our community

achieve its aims and receive its own justice. This community has lost some of its best and finest leaders in their finest hour. Let the violence stop now.'

A new voice came over the airwaves. It was Berniece Able, her strong seventy-year old voice ringing out with more wisdom than any statement Renquist could have made.

'History – there is no disaster – Those who make history – Cannot be overtaken – As they will make – History which they do – because it is necessary – That every one will – Begin to know that – They must know that – History is what it is – Which it is as they do – .'

I knew who the murderer was now. As I went over the facts of Tracy's and Deborah Dunton's murder I knew that what united them was beyond their gender and position in life. I didn't think that Renquist was in any danger. In fact, I thought that the whole series of murders, of Tracy, of Gurl Jesus, of Deborah, were to protect Renquist and further his career.

I waded through a sea of debris, floes that were once department store windows, cars whose tires had been burned, slashed. It had been an evening of white hot anger but now the coals had grown cold.

There would be fury and fallout, retribution and rebellion in the days to come. Many believed that the assassin Jeb Flynne was alive, protected by the Federal Government.

When I arrived at the St Francis I used my press pass at the hotel and got Homicide Inspector Ed Korian on the house phone to meet me at Falkenberg's suite. It was very easy. All I had to tell him was that I had proof of who had had access to the notes from Jeb Flynne. Who had mailed them to Tracy Port, to the police, and to the Supervisor.

Korian came in storm-trooper style. I followed him up to the suite, not exactly blending in with the crowd. He scowled at me as I crammed into the elevator with the uniforms, then filed out with them and stood in the hallway while Korian gave a few whispered instructions to his team.

'You're taking me in there with you,' I said.

'Hell I am.'

'*I* figured it out. *I* got shot. I'm going in with you.'

Could it have been that Korian smiled? Not a chance.

'At your own risk, Victor.'

And that's how I came into the Imperial Suite of the St Francis Hotel. Behind the drawn gun of Inspector Korian. That ridiculous drawn gun. As if he were facing someone very dangerous. Much more dangerous than the coward who was there.

Past a vestibule I saw the back of a couch. The cold light of a television played over the features of Allen Boone and Renquist Falkenberg.

Allen was squeezing Renquist's palm between both his hands. Korian coughed politely, as he crept up on the duo. Then he strolled in front of the couch and grabbed the frightened man's wrists, snapping the cuffs on.

'Allen Boone, I am arresting you on three counts of first degree murder. You have the right to remain silent, you have the right to an attorney, anything you say can and will be used against you in a court of law . . . '

Chapter Twenty

Twin Peaks

It was 9 pm. I was sitting in Rose's van on top of Twin Peaks. We looked down upon the city. A big smudge smoldered in the middle of it. Through Rose's windshield we stretched our eyes across the aqua bay. Mount Diablo was a black dinosaur on the horizon.

'How'd you know it was Allen Boone, Emma?'

'I was only really sure when I heard the notes of Jeb Flynne were popping up with regularity. It seemed so unlikely that Flynne could be alive, so I thought about who might have access to those threatening notes.

'When I saw a photo of the baptism I noticed Allen Boone. That was the first day Flynne sent one of his notes. Boone was present in many other photographs. And I had been in his office. The guy saved napkins, everything. He had boxes and boxes of stuff.

'And I'd clicked that Renquist had had an affair with Tracy. She was pregnant – I knew when I found the fragment of leftover pregnancy test in her bathroom bin. It was positive. I remembered all those jogging expeditions with Renquist, I remembered him calling her "dear" at the Archive Gala Dinner.

'I remembered finding condoms in his wallet. And condoms kept in wallets develop holes.'

'Oh, la, la . . .' Rose breathed.

'Allen must have gotten wind of it. You can imagine what he felt. Allen, the man who liked to be so close to history.

Renquist must have had the occasional fling with a woman. He kept things casual with Allen, never quite acknowledging him as a public partner. Meanwhile, Allen was collecting napkins, memorabilia from every gala, brunch and reception. He was always there, not wanting to be in the limelight himself but wanting to be in the thick of things.

'If he lost Renquist Falkenberg he'd be just another librarian. And it looked like he might be losing him. To Tracy Port. His boss. His overly officious boss. Behind the scenes, Allen must have been watching Tracy Port with mounting jealousy. And then he saw his opportunity. Helen Thomas' manuscripts.

'He encouraged Helen to donate them, to bring them, in fact, to the Gala that evening. Of course, nothing would set off Tracy worse than that. The Board had been so slow in developing admissions policy, her hands were tied. And she had the entire gala dinner to host, all those VIPs waiting.

'I was Allen's perfect witness. It was a marvelously staged argument. Poor Helen and her cyanide amulet. I suppose it is possible that Helen's necklace had poison in it. But hardly likely that a poison would remain viable for ninety years. Still, it looked good at the time, amidst the hugs and congratulations and bad food, Allen must have slipped Helen's necklace off. A few drops of poison in Tracy's potatoes, and a drop on Helen's necklace. *Voilà*. Instant cozy murder scene. And Helen the perfect suspect.

'But what Allen hadn't counted on was the photographer, Gurl Jesus, who had captured one of the moments on film. I don't know what she had, but I may have a negative of it somewhere. A moment where Allen pulled at something on Helen's neck? A moment where his hand hovers over Tracy's plate? Gurl called him. Her big card, of course, was that she would tell Renquist unless Allen paid her off. But Allen needed to keep Renquist – that was what it had all been about. He would have been absolutely desperate so he shot Gurl Jesus through the back.'

'And Deborah Dunton? How'd she get in the way?'

'Deborah had called a meeting to discuss Tracy's memorial. I don't think she liked Allen. She invited Renquist and myself, leaving out the deputy archivist who had never liked Tracy anyway.

'Allen was starting to freak. He was convinced that Deborah knew. Remember, Allen read every newspaper in the city, the two dailies, and the four weeklies. And he knew there had been a well-publicized shotgun murder in the Mews complex. He decided he had to get to Deborah before Renquist did.'

'And he almost got you in the process.'

'But Deborah was close to the truth. I don't think she would have fooled . herself that much longer about Lee Turgo. In fact, I think Deborah had pretty strong suspicions about Tracy's pregnancy.'

'What makes you think so?'

'She'd stolen Frances' *Lesbo-Parthenogenesis* notes. She must have taken them at the Archive dinner – I admit I was pretty careless with them. I suppose she thought they might contain some sort of insemination records including Tracy Port – But of course, they didn't.

'In any case, Allen came calling, not thinking I would be there so early. Perhaps he overheard Deborah talking about Tracy in the hallway. He went into the gun case, pried off the lock and took one of the guns. He followed our voices down the hallway.

'My suspicion is that he knew all along that the guns were there. Deborah was always holding those dreadful benefit brunches. He is very likely to have been at some of them, or to have heard about the guns from someone who was.

'After killing Gurl Jesus, Allen must have been thinking double-time. That's where he tripped up. He veered away from the Helen Thomas motive. He was afraid someone would make the connection with Gurl Jesus and the Gala. He had the notes of Jeb Flynne, the original threatening notes written in the name of the Family Values Society. Murder. Blood. Shame. Guilt. It was all in Jeb Flynne's notes.'

'I feel completely bloodied? Jeb Flynne wrote that?' Rose was incredulous.

'Yes, he did. He was an extreme right-wing fundamentalist remember. The whole concept of baptising the children of homosexuals attacked his religion, his way of life. He felt "bloodied" by the whole experience.

'Allen slipped into Tracy's room and simply threw a fragment of one of Flynne's notes on the floor, where someone was definitely sure to find it. He watched as I picked it up.'

'He was in the apartment while you were there? With shotgun in hand?'

'Waiting for Deborah. Who surprised me in the bathroom. The gunshot came from the bedroom and blasted her apart in front of my eyes. Allen hit my shoulder. If I'd caught sight of him, I suppose he would have killed me too.'

'Oh Emma.' Rose put her hand on my shoulder. 'Thank God you're sitting here beside me in the van, not spread all over Tracy Port's floor.'

I didn't want to dwell on the possibility.

'Then Allen started up a real campaign to convince everyone that Flynne was alive. He sent notes. Too many notes. Flynne's notes were sporadic, in response to a perceived ideological threat that could ruin his life. He just wasn't a murder and mayhem kind of guy. The police didn't believe them.'

Rose's eyes reflected the moon which had just risen over the crest of Mount Diablo. 'How does Carla Ribera fit into all this?'

I said nothing. I wasn't going to tell Rose that Carla Ribera's politics were more radical than we could have imagined. That Carla may be involved in an international organisation to protect underground radicals. That maybe the fashion photography and the long-legged models *were* just a pose. That Carla still loved Rose. No, I wouldn't stick my finger into that mess.

'Well, Emma, all I can say is I'm glad you're still around.'

Rose started the engine and took me home, where I turned off the phone and slept for a good ten hours.

Chapter Twenty-One

What Eleanor Roosevelt Said

I had been standing in front of the Archive since seven forty-five, holding on to a safety deposit key which had come in the mail yesterday morning.

Standing wasn't accurate. I'd been walking, sitting, chewing on my fingernails. Waiting for her. Taking note of all the cars, pedestrians, loiterers like myself. Holding that key. Looking for her. Everything looked copacetic. Safe. So where was she?

I lurked behind the windows of laundromats. Doing everything that might make me inconspicuous enough to be approachable. At 9 am I gave up. At ten I felt foolish. The sea gulls were laughing at me now. It was time to go home. San Francisco was too hot a town for Fresca Alcazon. That was all.

When I got back to my apartment I found Frances' Miyata parked in front of the apartment. The hood was up, the engine was warm. And the back seat was full of luggage. Somehow, I had known.

I slipped quietly into the apartment. A lot of Frances' back was showing through a deep V cut in a beige cotton dress. She was running the blender. There was an empty vermouth bottle by her elbow and the triangular Martini glass in front of her. I watched the swing of her hips, the tapping of her foot. When the blender stopped I watched her pour the mixed Martini into the glass and lift it to her lips as she stared out the kitchen window. She would need that drink when she realized I was standing right behind her. Finally, I said something. She jumped and dropped the glass.

'Emma!'

'Little early isn't it?'

'Emma, my God I didn't know you were – don't ever –' And then Frances stopped and looked at me and if I had any doubts left, they were gone.

'Don't ever what?'

'Sneak up on me!' She looked angry but only for a second. 'Hey, you got your nose pierced,' she said wanly.

'You like it?'

'Yeah!' She cocked her head and laughed in a strangled way. 'I do like it.' She sounded like her heart was breaking. 'Emma, oh Emma, I – I don't know how to tell you this –'

'You're leaving me aren't you?'

We stared at the broken glass on the floor. Somewhere a car honked and in the distance school children were screaming.

'Yes. I'm leaving you.'

How to hold on to tears, face, lips. I looked out into the garden. I buried my feelings there in the warm, black, fetid soil.

'I don't really want any answers,' I managed to say. I'd forgotten that I hadn't asked any questions.

'Yes. Let's not –'

'But Frances, on the other hand, I don't want to make it *too* easy –'

'Please?' Frances asked quietly. 'Don't.'

'Well, who is she?'

'Let's not do that either.'

'You're leaving me after five years?'

'We haven't been close for a long time.'

'Hey, *you* kept *me* on ice, remember?'

'Emma, let's not.'

'I knew you'd say that.'

'Yeah, I knew I would say it too.' She smiled. It made me angry.

'I suppose you're trading me in for an upscale model, something in government, perhaps?'

'Emma, sarcasm isn't going to help.'

'Well, it's helping me right now.'

'I want to leave now, Emma. This serves no purpose. We – we'll have to deal with the house; I'll pay the mortgage – '

Guilt money. There was a violent moment in my brain, but it was better to look out the window. I'd grow dinner plate dahlias this time. Big, fluffy white ones. Better camouflage.

'Emma?'

'What?'

'Do you want me to apologize?'

'Huh?'

'Do you want me to apologize?' She repeated more quietly.

'Will it make you feel better?' There were sticky weeds crawling from under the neighbor's fence. The kind of weeds that get caught in cats' tails. Were we going to split up the cats?

'I'm sorry, Emma. I really am.'

There was a long pause and then Frances asked 'Didn't make *you* feel better, did it?' She was crying now. I could hear it in her voice.

'Nope.' I shook my head. A swallowtail butterfly floated along the marguerites.

'Goodbye, Emma.' And then I listened to Frances' foot-steps going across the newly cleaned floor, down the stairs, avoiding the squeaky tread which she had done so many times.

Then I went back into my apartment, my very own apartment and searched under the guestroom bed. I found the bud of the plant that Fresca had failed to drown and located some cigarette papers.

Twenty minutes later I was sitting in the garden, feeling

that glorious California sunlight with all its UV rays shining on my skin. I took a long toke, and surveyed the garden. Butterflies and blackberry vines. Something that Eleanor Roosevelt had said came to me: After forty, everything bad has happened once.

Certain truths were self-evident.

My heart was broken and I was sitting in the sun planning next year's fauna.

I'd had a weekend of heartbreak, murder and mayhem. My nose was pierced. I was the proud owner of a Stein first edition.

Frances was, in some way, leaving me.

I would get beyond it.

I would see Fresca Alcazon again. And she would have the other key.

And I truly believed that every woman in this dyke life must have a *garden*.